DOG OPERA

by

CONSTANCE CONGDON

SAMUEL FRENCH, INC.

45 WEST 25TH STREET   NEW YORK 10010

7623 SUNSET BOULEVARD HOLLYWOOD 90046

LONDON   TORONTO

IMPORTANT BILLING AND CREDIT REQUIREMENTS

All producers of DOG OPERA *must* give credit to the Author of the Play in all programs distributed in connection with performances of the Play and in all instances in which the title of the Play appears for purposes of advertising, publicizing or otherwise exploiting the Play and/or a production. The name of the Author *must* also appear on a separate line, on which no other name appears, immediately following the title, and *must* appear in size of type not less than fifty percent the size of the title type.

Original New York Production by
The New York Shakespeare Festival,
George C. Wolfe, Producer

CAST
(In Order of Appearance)

Peter Szczepanek ....ALBERT MACKLIN

Madeline Newell ....KRISTINE NIELSEN

Jackie ....KEVIN DEWEY

Steven/Chris/David/
Tim/Hank ....RICK HOLMES

Bernice/Ruby/Dale Williamson/
Doris/Maureen ....SLOANE SHELTON

Joe's Lover/Man on the Street/
Stavros/Paul/Arapahoe ....EDUARDO ANDINO

Charlie Szczepanek/
Brad/Sanny ....RICHARD RUSSELL RAMOS

CHARACTER DESCRIPTIONS

PETER SZCZEPANEK—thirty-five plus, insecure about his looks, secure about his homosexuality, vulnerable, very VERY funny, good blue-collar Catholic boy raised in Queens who made the very long trip into Manhattan to have an interesting life. Madeline's best friend since he was 14.

MADELINE NEWELL—thirty-five plus, insecure about her looks, chubby or more, heterosexual, very VERY funny, good blue-collar Catholic girl raised in Queens who made the very long trip into Manhattan to go to NYU so she could have an interesting life. Peter's best friend since she was 14.

CHARLIE SZCZEPANEK—fifty-eight or so, about to retire from the NYPD where he's had a desk job after 20 years as a homicide detective and ten years on the beat. A widower of several years and Peter's father. He got married in 1958, at the age of 22 or so, after coming back from the Korean War.

BERNICE NEWELL—early sixties, not in good health, but irascible and matter-of-fact. A "tough old broad." Madeline's mother, still living in Queens in the apartment Madeline was raised in.

JACKIE—a teenager, 17 years old, from the Midwest, on the street for a year of so, a hooker who dances to taped music from a beat box while clients jerk off. Ingenuous.

STEVEN—an anal, cheerful "date" of Peter's.

JOE'S LOVER--30+, speaks at Joe's memorial service.

CHRIS—an old boyfriend of Peter's, now quite ill.

DAVID—a flirty male teacher who works with Madeline at the elementary school and pretends to be heterosexual.

BRAD—a waiter at Peter's favorite bar (a place like the Town House) called The Morocco.

RUBY—an older transvestite who also works at The Morocco.

TIM—a really nice guy who becomes Peter's lover for a while.

HANK—a one-time boyfriend of Madeline's that she thought she was cured of. Would rather watch football than have sex, but would never admit it. Jealous of Peter but hides it.

STAVROS—Greek man who lives on Mykonos and sleeps with the tourists (gay males his preference), but occasionally falls in love and means it for a while.

DALE WILLIAMSON—from Duluth, Minnesota and in her fifties, she's traveling with a group of Americans--single and looking for fun.

DORIS—and older gay woman, forty-five or so, who is alone and goes to the girl bar to pick someone up. Well-dressed, not particularly butch.

SANNY—an old guy of questionable sexuality who's lived in Brooklyn all his life--sounds like Bill Hickey.

ARAPAHOE—a beautiful Native American (Arapahoe) man who's been circling the earth for a long time, carrying souls of the dying and just-dead. He loves his job--it gives him peace.

CHARACTERS
{2W; 5M}

This play works best with an ensemble of actors playing several roles, with the exception of JACKIE, MADELINE, PETER. The actors playing these three characters should not double.

MOTHER (BERNICE) ACTOR:
Bernice, Ruby, Dale, Doris, perhaps, Sanny

BOYFRIEND (TIM) ACTOR:
Steven, Chris, David, Hank, Tim

BOYFRIEND (STAVROS) ACTOR:
Joe's Lover, Stavros, Man (Gay Street), Arapahoe

CHARLIE ACTOR:
Charlie, Brad, Sanny (if the MOTHER actor doesn't do it)

SETTING
New York City and environs, in the present, and, briefly, in Greece.

STAGING
The staging should be very fluid and avoid blackouts--even the ones I've asked for.

Let me not to the marriage of true minds
Admit impediments. Love is not love
Which alters when it alteration finds,
Or bends with the remover to remove:
O, no! it is an ever-fixed mark,
That looks on tempests and is never shaken;
It is the star to every wandering bark,
Whose worth's unknown, although his height be taken.
Love's not Time's fool, though rosy lips and cheeks
Within his bending sickle's compass come;
Love alters not with his brief hours and weeks,
But bears it out even to the edge of doom.
If this be error, and upon me prov'd,
I never writ, nor no man ever lov'd.

William Shakespeare
Sonnet CXVI

For Greg Leaming

ACT I

(PETE and MADELINE are semi-reclining in aluminum chaises on a public beach. They are wearing t-shirts, hats, sunglasses and towels over their thighs. They are sharing a can of Diet Coke.)

PETE. There's just one thing...
MADELINE. What?
PETE. One thing I'm worried about.
MADELINE. What?
PETE. Will guys think I'm a transsexual?
MADELINE. You're too hairy.
PETE. Hormones can do that. It's this towel.
MADELINE. Take it off.
PETE. And let the world see my thighs? I don't think so.
MADELINE. *Your* thighs?
PETE. Don't start.
MADELINE. If Green Peace were here, I'd be on the news tonight--"Twin Orcas beached on Long Island." *(Sees a guy.)* Oh man.
PETE. They're fine. You're fine.
MADELINE. No, I mean, "Oh." "Man."
PETE. Where?
MADELINE. At three o'clock.
PETE. Now--wait a minute. Where is midnight?
MADELINE. Straight ahead.
PETE. And six is back here.

11

MADELINE. You're going to miss him.

PETE. Where?

MADELINE. I'm not pointing. Forget it.

PETE. *(Thinks he spies the guy.)* Oh, wait a minute. Blue speedos?

MADELINE. Grey.

PETE. If you're quibbling about the color, how great can this guy be?

MADELINE. You missed him.

PETE. *(Sees another guy.)* Whoa, doggies.

MADELINE. What is this? Jed Clampett cruises Jones Beach?

PETE. Lord have mercy.

MADELINE. *(Sees this guy.)* Oh my.

PETE. Ohhhh. Ohhhhh. Mama.

MADELINE. A basket worthy of Carmen Miranda's head.

PETE. She'll have to fight me for him.

MADELINE. Buns.

PETE. Buns.

(MADELINE and PETE take him in.)

MADELINE. Gay.

PETE. Straight. *(Reconsidering.)* Straight.

MADELINE. Gay.

PETE. Acid test: invite him over.

MADELINE. If I fall in love with him--he's gay.

PETE. If I fall in love with him--he's straight. *(Weakly.)* Oh sir? Sir? Can you come over here and ruin our lives?

MADELINE. Oh please, it's been at least two weeks.

PETE. Oh my god.

MADELINE. What?

PETE. He's looking at us.

MADELINE. Oh jeez.

PETE. I'm going to take off my towel.

MADELINE. That should do it.

PETE. What's that supposed to mean?

MADELINE. Peter, take off the towel.

(PETE takes his towel off--he's wearing a long pair of black bathing trunks.)

MADELINE Those *are* fetching.

PETE. He's coming over, Madeline! Oh fuck.

MADELINE. Will you relax?

PETE. He's looking at me.

MADELINE. I knew he was gay. He's motioning...

PETE. I've attracted a deaf-mute. It'll be like Children of a Lesser God. Oh my god! I'm Bill Hurt! *(To guy.)* What? Oh, no, I don't have any--sorry! I quit six months ago. *(He watches guy exit.)* But I'd be glad to make you one if you bring me the tobacco! *(Guy is gone.)* Or just bring me your seeds and we'll grow it together. Or if you have a gun, I'd be glad to shoot myself in the other foot. *(PETE sits down.)* I'm sure he appreciated the lecture on quitting smoking.

MADELINE. It wasn't a lecture. It was a comment.

PETE. He was gay, Madeline. And he almost talked to me until I turned into Bobby Bizarro.

MADELINE. Pete--he was straight.

PETE. How do you know?

MADELINE. If he were gay, he would have talked to me, too.

PETE. You're right. I wasn't just rejected.

MADELINE. You weren't just rejected.

PETE. I was asked for a cigarette. And I didn't have any.

MADELINE. That simple. *(Long beat.)* I was rejected. He didn't even talk to me. I don't know--maybe the towel makes me look fatter.

PETE. Take it off.

MADELINE. When pigs fly. *(Beat.)* When pigs fly, maybe I'll join the air force--at last, a suit that fits me.

PETE. Stop it. I like that black thing you bought.

MADELINE. Which black thing? All my clothes are black.

PETE. The dressy suit thing.

MADELINE. Oh, my memorial outfit?

PETE. I guess so.

MADELINE. It's ten years old! I bought it for... Barry.

PETE. Barry. Barry's memorial. That's an old suit.

MADELINE. Too old. Burn it. Take it out and burn it. I need a new suit, Peter.

PETE. Me, too. Hey! Hey, hey, hey! What are we doin'?

MADELINE. We are cruisin'. We are strategically placed just to the left of Field Six at Jones Beach, so the pickins' are great.

PETE. And the livin' is easy.

MADELINE. Straight men to the left of me.

PETE. Gay men to the right of me.

MADELINE. Into the valley of... *life* rode the six hundred.

PETE. And that's why there are no cute guys— Six hundred hunky light brigade officers rode up—

MADELINE. And took the cute ones— *(Sees a guy.)* —wait a minute. Nine o'clock. Approaching—

PETE. Now, where's nine again?

MADELINE. *(Showing him quickly.)* Noon, Three. Six. Nine.

PETE. *(Sees him.)* Very attractive black man?

MADELINE. Red speedos.

PETE. Oh my god. Remind me to make an offering to the god of nylon.

MADELINE. All synthetic fibers aren't bad.

(PETE and MADELINE watch him.)

PETE. Well, that made my afternoon.

MADELINE. Yeah.

(MADELINE is still watching as he disappears down the beach.)

PETE. Gay? Straight?

MADELINE. Beautiful.

(End of Scene)

(JACKIE, a young effeminate teenager, is waiting on a highway for a ride. It's a beautiful dusk evening—the sound of crickets. We see a few fireflies.)

JACKIE. Crickets make that sound by rubbing their parts together—they're trying to get a date of some kind. They're also eating spiders as they do this. It's a beautiful night. Fireflies are mooning each other. They die in a few weeks. In the grass and trees, insect life is trying to overpopulate in between doing search and destroy attacks on each other. Once this whole state was a swamp and dinosaurs sloshed around. Now their decay could ignite a fire fifty feet high. Trees died to make those houses. And under all of this is a layer of dead Indians. If motel rooms didn't have cable, I wouldn't know any of this, and I'd be a lot happier. Everyone says I'm smart and I shoulda stayed in school. Well, yeah. Where would I have lived, I wonder? I have some skills—I can put on a condom with my teeth, before the guy even realizes it's there. Mostly, I jerk off to music of my choice. I take requests, but I will not do "People" by Barbra Streisand or anything of a religious nature. *(Looking down the street.)* Here they come—on their way home from work, in their big dark cars with the ample backseats. But I won't be getting in—even wrapped in latex. I have a date tonight. With somebody's husband—yours? *(Sees car pulling up.)* Oh my god. He brought the station wagon—with the kid's car seat still in the back. No graham cracker crumbs on this boy—we're getting a room!

(He waves to the driver and exits to get into the car.)

(end of scene)

(Soft, meditative music and ocean sound. MADELINE has her eyes closed and is wearing earphones. We are listening to what she hears.)

WOMAN'S VOICE. Breathing doubt out,
Breathing hope in,

Don't stop breathing.
It feels good to relax and breathe.
Notice what you're thinking
And observe your thoughts
Without judging them
There's no such thing as a bad thought
Or a better thought
thoughts are just thoughts,
Nothing more, nothing less.

(As MADELINE'S tape continues, PETE enters in a separate space. He is wearing a bathrobe and jockey shorts and nothing else. He crosses to an attractive little box, opens it and puts three unopened condoms in it and shuts the lid.)

All your thoughts are valuable
Because they give you useful information
And they help you to understand and accept
Your total self.
So even though your thoughts might be
Illogical, unreasonable or untrue,
They're just thoughts,
They're not actions.

(PETE picks up the phone and thinks about dialing.)

Put aside your thoughts one by one
As your body relaxes
Take a mental vacation
Let your conscious mind ramble on and on
While your higher self takes over.

(PETE watches as a man wearing only a pair of jockey shorts, earphones and a cassette player in the crotch of his shorts, crosses through, mopping the floor as he goes. This is STEVEN.)

WOMAN'S VOICE. Trust in the compassion of your
            higher self
And its wisdom.
Listen to it.
You use food only to nourish your body
Food is not love
Love is love
Food is not a reward

(MADELINE reaches for a bag of Oreos. She can't find them and begins to search with real energy. PETE dials the phone.)

A reward is emotional satisfaction
So reward yourself in positive, healthy ways
Because you deserve to be loved.

(As the taped message continues, MADELINE finds the oreos.)

You are getting comfort and companionship
In healthy and constructive ways.

(MADELINE puts an oreo in her mouth—it is bliss. Phone rings. She turns off the cassette and picks up the phone receiver.)

PETE. Are you alone?

MADELINE. Oh, no, the L.A. Raiders are over here. They're fucking my brains out. Unfortunately, I'm in the other room, because, like all men on the planet, they only want me FOR MY MIND!

PETE. Since you're awake, anyway.

MADELINE. Of course I'm awake. I ran out of batteries for all my sex toys an hour ago.

PETE. Take some out of your cassette player.

MADELINE. Wrong size.

PETE. Remember—size doesn't matter.

MADELINE. It's been so long—do they come in different sizes? I forgot. Wait a minute—you had a date.

PETE. That was a rumor.

MADELINE. Oh no.

PETE. Oh yes.

MADELINE. So he cancelled?

PETE. No. He came—arrived. What does it mean when they clean your house?

MADELINE. In my case, it means they should be going out with *you.*

PETE. What would it mean in my case? I thought I was dating my own kind. I'm not straight. Evidently, I'm not gay because if I were I would be HAVING GAY SEX, RIGHT?!!! So what am I—a fucking amoeba? I mean, what am I—a fucking chromosome? What am I supposed to do, huh? Split in two discreet pieces, say "Ah!" and then have a cigarette? And worry if I'm going to call myself the next day? Wait a minute—Hazel, the celibate maid, is coming around again.

(STEVEN re-enters, carrying a spray bottle and a sponge, and humming to the cassette player.)

STEVEN. *(Too loud because he can't hear.)* FOUND SOME MURPHY'S SOAP—GONNA DO THE WALLS TOO. THIS PANELLING IS FABULOUS. YOU SHOULDN'T NEGLECT IT.

(STEVEN cleans with great concentration.)

MADELINE. Why is Hazel shouting? Does celibacy make you deaf? See, our mothers had it all wrong.

PETE. Why does every weird homo in the world want to date me?

MADELINE. I don't know, Peter. You're too normal. You're like the Statue of Liberty—"Give me your weird ones, your refugees from too much therapy. Send these, the retro queens who still think their mothers made them a homosexual, and are gathering wool so their mothers can make them another."

PETE. I lift my lamp and go door to door: "DATE ME, I'm HOPELESS!"

MADELINE. What happened?

(STEVEN bends over to clean and the butt shot is too much for PETE to bear.)

PETE. Uhhhh.

MADELINE. Are you all right?

PETE. I'm alive. *(Vincent Price arising from the grave.)* I'm ALIVE!"

MADELINE. No nooky, then?

PETE. No. Nope on the nooky. Wants to be friends. Needs a friend. Wants a friend. Had too much meaningless sex! Worried about AIDS. Needs companionship. "GM wants to meet other GM for walks on the beach, long dinners and lots of talk"—in short, anything you can do with your MOTHER!

MADELINE. With *my* mother? Only if you bring a walker. And that rubber donut she's sat on since 1986. And a bottle of Canadian Club. *(Beat.)* You still there?

PETE. I'm watching the floor show.

STEVEN. I FEEL SO AT HOME HERE, PAUL!!

PETE. Pete. My name's—MY NAME'S PETE!! *PETER!*

STEVEN. MAYBE LATER IN THE RELATIONSHIP! I WANT TO REDISCOVER MY VIRGINITY! HA! HA! BUT IN THE MEANTIME, THIS APARTMENT IS GONNA BE *CLEAN!*

(STEVEN goes back to cleaning.)

PETE. I have to go now—I have to go open a vein.

MADELINE. Make sure it's his. Wait. Did you actually get anywhere?

PETE. Nope.

MADELINE. Not even mutual pud pulling or anything?

PETE. Oh, you old romantic, you.

MADELINE. Well, "Masturbation" sounds like something we did in high school chemistry. "Now, students, carefully masturbate your pipettes and be certain you get none of it in your mouths."

PETE. Sister Mary Joseph was ahead of her time.

MADELINE. I can't stand it! Did you or didn't you!!?

PETE. I had that little problem again, but it had nothing to do with "Hazel's" telling me about his "vocation." *(Long pause.)* Aren't you going to say it happens to every man now and then?

MADELINE. How would I know? The entire fucking

world could be impotent and I wouldn't know the difference!

PETE. Don't say "impotent."

MADELINE. You're not, Pete. You are not. It's just a temporary thing. If you were faced with someone really hot who wasn't afraid, you know it would all be there.

PETE. I'm dying.

MADELINE. No, you're not.

(Pause.)

PETE. All right.

MADELINE. Bye, Pete.

PETE. And don't eat the rest of those Oreos, Madeline. You know what chocolate does to you.

MADELINE. Yeah—makes me happy. *(Beat.)* All right.

PETE. Movies on Friday?

MADELINE. Right. Your choice, god help me.

PETE. Bye, Maddy.

MADELINE. Bye.

(PETE and MADELINE hang up. MADELINE smiles and puts the Oreos away.)

STEVEN. I LOVE THIS SONG! I'M GOING TO PLAY IT AGAIN! *(He reaches into his jockey shorts and reverses the tape and then starts it again.)* GOD! I LOVE THIS SONG!!!

(STEVEN dances off. PETER lies back down in bed.)

(end of scene)

(BERNICE, MADELINE'S mother, enters, walking with her walker, heading for her chair. It's a big recliner with a chairside cabinet on which rests a small refrigerator. She gets there, sits.)

BERNICE. Damn. *(She gets up slightly and takes a large rubber donut from her chair seat, rearranges it and sits back down. She picks up her tv remote and flicks through the channels—stops at something—)* Now, what in god's name is that? *(Flicks more—finds a disaster program like "Code 3". She likes this litany of disaster, opens her refrigerator, takes out an already-prepared highball and takes a taste. Then she takes out a bottle of Canadian Club and pours some on her drink, sips it, then really downs a slug of it.)* Perfect. *(She turns up the volume on the disaster program, then turns it down.)* Shit. I gotta go to the toilet. *(BERNICE gets up and walks off with her walker. Beat. BERNICE yells offstage.)* ACK!! *(We hear a big thump.)* GODDAMMIT!! MADELINE!!!!!!

(end of scene)

(Celestial music. MADELINE is sitting next to an empty chair. PETE stands behind her. They are both bathed in white, listening to the music. When they talk, their VOICEOVERS are a little off, so it seems they are in a dubbed movie.)

MADELINE. This music...
PETE. So beautiful.
MADELINE. This is the most beautiful memorial—
PETE.—anyone could imagine. You know why?

MADELINE. No.
PETE. It's because it's the last one.

(PETE starts to leave.)

MADELINE. You mean, there's a cur—
PETE. No, we're finally all dead.

(PETE is gone.)

MADELINE. *(Waking suddenly, terrified.)* Wha!? Pete!
MAN'S OFFSTAGE VOICE FROM PODIUM. —and the
hospice people who were so wonderful to Joe and me.
*(MADELINE calms herself and hopes no one saw that she
was asleep, looks at her watch and then behind her, worried.)* Once the Catholic Church rejected me, I never looked
back, but today, I'd like to offer a special silent prayer to all
of the souls that I feel are around us—to thank them for their
help because I know they're here, today, sharing our memo-
ries of Joe. We're all one community, the living and the dead,
and I believe that all of our friends and lovers are still with
us.

*(MADELINE looks behind once more, then bows her head.
PETE enters, breathless; and sits beside her.)*

PETE. Sorry.
MADELINE. Thank God.
PETE. Tough one?
MADELINE. You're sweating.
PETE. I had to run for a cab. I told them I had to leave

early. They knew I was coming here. And still George kept droning on and on. Oh, God, are we supposed to be praying? Shit.

(PETE bows his head. We see the source of the OFFSTAGE MALE VOICE. It is JOE'S LOVER.)

JOE'S LOVER. Amen. Joe's mother and I want to thank you all for coming. He wanted me to read this today, whenever today came. He kept this piece of paper by his bed. He'd found this saying in a book of Native American writings and copied it out for himself, so he could read it any time. Later, he had me read it to him. It's Arapahoe. "Every time I go about pitying myself or despairing for the lives of my people, I remember that I am being carried on great winds across the sky." Good-bye, Joe.

(Classical music. MADELINE and PETE sit there. After a beat, they wave weakly to someone they recognize. Then they see someone else and wave. They do this a bit more.)

MADELINE. You know, it just gets harder and harder to get out of these seats.

PETE. I still think Allen's was the best memorial in a long time.

MADELINE. This one was good—great music, since Joe was a musician, but not as many stories, you know—outrageous stories, like at Allen's.

PETE. Oh, god, has it killed outrageous, too? Left us only outrage?

MADELINE. Joe was younger, that's all. Shorter life.

PETE. Uh-oh.
MADELINE. Uh-oh.
PETE. Right. Right. Right.
MADELINE. Out of here.

(MADELINE and PETE get up to go.)

PETE. You didn't know Bill? Or Joe's mom?
MADELINE. You mean, do we have to say anything to anyone?
PETE. Right.
MADELINE. We met Joe at the same time, didn't we?
Through Don at that—a—
PETE. Through Kevin.
MADELINE. Oh god, Kevin. Of course.

(PETE and MADELINE see someone else they know and wave. Upstage, a man appears, walking with those aluminum crutches that are braced with the forearm. He is sick, but looks okay—his clothes are big on him. This is CHRIS.)

CHRIS. Peter?

(PETE turns around, sees him.)

PETE. Oh my god.
CHRIS. It's Chris.
PETE. Oh my god. Hello. How—

(PETE stops himself.)

CHRIS. I moved back months ago, but I didn't call you. I

couldn't stay in Texas. I hated it. I should've called, but you know—I thought you'd still be pissed.

PETE. No. Not at all. Well, I was, but...

CHRIS. Listen, I've still got your mother's afghan. I'm living with Jerry. Olsen, you know.

PETE. Oh my god.

CHRIS. So, call me and come pick it up. Sometime. *(To MADELINE.)* You must be the famous Madeline.

MADELINE. Right. You must be the famous Chris.

CHRIS. Infamous—please. *(To PETE.)* Don't wait too long—asshole. *(CHRIS turns to go, has trouble with the crutches.)* Rugs are death with these things.

MADELINE. Let me help.

CHRIS. I got it.

(CHRIS exits.)

PETE. Jesus.
MADELINE. Peter?

(PETE sits down. A long beat.)

PETE. Jesus. Chris. Jesus. Jesus.
MADELINE. Pete?
PETE. It's been four years since Chris. I am negative.
MADELINE. I know that.
PETE. And, let's face it, with my love life—there's no threat. I have to sit for a moment.

MADELINE. *(About PETE'S health.)* You're sweating.

PETE. I ran for the cab. *(Gentle but adamant.)* I— ran — for the cab.

MADELINE. That's right. I forgot. Sorry.
PETE. Let's get out of here.

(PETE and MADELINE exit quickly.)

(end of scene)

(JACKIE is in a motel room, watching the television. There's the sound of a shower running.)

JACKIE. He has to get home, but I get to keep the room. I love it. A double all to myself. People make fun of motel rooms—say they all look alike, but it's only the nice ones that do. Crummy motel rooms are always different because no one has decorated them in a modern fashion, so they are stuck in whatever time they were built. Ones built in the Seventies have shag carpeting and fake wood beams and they're orange and brown. The Eighties were about silver and geometric designs. And mirrors. Lots of them. The Nineties? They're not crummy yet. Now this room has a strip of carpet that runs up the wall between two fake wood beams. And the wallpaper's flocked. I think they call that eclectic. *(Tries to change the channel.)* Fuck! This remote is fucked! *(Opens his bag and pours out lots of remotes. He tries them, one by one.)* No. No. No. Nope. Shit! *(One of the remotes works.)* Thank god. You know how most remotes are in these bracket holder things that are bolted to the bedside tables in motels? It's because of me. *(Switches channels as he talks.)* Now nice motels, like Budgetel, Days Inn, Travelodge, they do all look alike—the rooms. But I love that. Because, when I walk into one, I feel as though I've just

walked into an apartment of my own. I don't get many of those
dates, but, when I do, I always take the miniature shampoo
and conditioners and sometimes they have handcream and
good brands like Vaseline Intensive Care. You ever noticed
shower caps? They come in all these different boxes—round
ones, and big flat ones, and little narrow ones, all different,
right? No, when you open one of these up, it's the same fucking
shower cap. Always, always, always.

NATURE PROGRAM VO. —have evolved extravagant
breeding plumage as sexual advertisements to attract their
mates. Long white plumes which this bird bears on its back in
the mating and nesting season have long been used for adorn-
ment, but this beautiful plumage can only be acquired by kill-
ing the animal.

JACKIE. Those are egrets. They're a very, very ancient bird.
And they almost died out. But they're not gone yet. They're
hanging in there.

NATURE PROGRAM VO. The delicately plumed Snowy
Egret with its yellow feet, called "golden slippers" is begin-
ning to repopulate Northern California where it originally suf-
fered great losses to the plume trade.

(end of scene)

(PETE is in his bathrobe, holding some videotapes.)

PETE. "Send Me A Few Hard Men. Discipline and hard-
core fun at a Marine boot camp." Maybe Gomer Pyle will be
in this one. *(Puts the tape in the VCR, settles back, fast for-
wards. In Gomer Pyle voice.)* "Sergeant Carter? Surprise,

surprise, surprise!" *(About the movie.)* Still dressed? What can this be? Plot?

MALE VOICE #2. You wanted me, Sarge?

MALE VOICE #1. Yes. Private. You could say that.

PETE. These guys are great actors.

MALE VOICE #2. What do you want me to do, Sarge?

PETE. Hello? Sir John Gielgud?

MALE VOICE #1. I think we both know the answer to that one.

PETE. You're fired.

MALE VOICE #1. Down on your knees, soldier!

PETE. *(Seeing the size of the film actor's dick.)* You're definitely fired. Sir John.

(PETE watches the videotape as the marching snare drum and groans take over. He tilts his head to the side, slowly, to see better. Phone rings. He picks up. Lights up on MADELINE calling from her apartment.)

MADELINE. Hi.

PETE. Hi.

MADELINE. Whatcha doin?

PETE. Watching a movie.

MADELINE. Oh great! What? I thought I'd drop by.

PETE. Uhhhhhhhhm.

MADELINE. Somebody's there. Cool.

PETE. *(Turns down the movie.)* No. Don't hang up.

MADELINE. What's the movie?

PETE. It's a—it's an educational film: an anthropological study of male bonding behavior among the inhabitants of a small military installation.

MADELINE. I'll let you go.
PETE. I'll turn it off.
MADELINE. No, Peter.
PETE. *HOW* CAN I DO ANYTHING KNOWING YOU
KNOW WHAT I'M DOING?
MADELINE. Call me later.

(MADELINE hangs up.)

PETE. Maddy! What if nothing happens again?

(PETE turns the volume up again. We hear the moans and more frantic snare drum.)

MALE VOICE #2. Do me, Daddy!
PETE. Yikes.

(PETE tries to relax and get into the movie again, hoping for arousal.)

MALE VOICE #2. Daddy, Daddy.
PETE. Stop with the dad stuff, for god's sake.

(Back to MADELINE. She dials the phone. It is picked up by CHARLIE, a middle-aged man in a suit.)

CHARLIE. Detective Szczepanek.
MADELINE. Bang.
CHARLIE. Maddy. Put that thing down. If I've told you once, I've told you a million times, a little girl like you can't handle those big guns.

MADELINE. I can hope, can't I?

CHARLIE. So what's the plan?

MADELINE. The Zen Palate.

CHARLIE. Oh god.

MADELINE. It's not *your* birthday. It's Peter's—your son.

CHARLIE. What's wrong with good old American food? Like in Chinatown, for godssake?

MADELINE. Peter loves the Zen Palate.

CHARLIE. I'll eat before I come.

MADELINE. What are you going to get him?

CHARLIE. I'm having his grandfather's ring resized for him.

MADELINE. The thirty-year ring? God, isn't that an antique.

CHARLIE. Thanks.

MADELINE. No, I mean, really, Charlie. Your dad was in the NYPD when they were chasing Al Capone.

CHARLIE. That was Chicago! Jesus! Your generation has no memory!

MADELINE. I'm sorry—I'm not up on gangster history. If, however, you'd like to discuss the role of the patron in Renaissance art—

CHARLIE. Throw your education up to me--fine. Let me tell you something, Madeline Newell. Renaissance art will only tell you what you aren't because you are an American. And Gangster history *is* American history. Your professors at NYU didn't tell you that. And you know why? Because *that* is the truth.

MADELINE. Charlie? Take two Midol and call me in the morning. Or, better yet, take the whole fucking bottle and don't call me.

CHARLIE. Now, don't get mad, Maddy.

MADELINE. Why do you always say that?

CHARLIE. Because you always get mad, Zelda. *(Pause.)* Getting any?

MADELINE. Mr. Szczepanek—

CHARLIE. Giving any away?

MADELINE. Charlie, I'm hanging up now.

CHARLIE. Hey, I like our exchange of ideas, you know? The word "renaissance" never comes up here--hardly. You didn't hang up, did you?

MADELINE. No.

CHARLIE. Ha, ha!

(CHARLIE hangs up the phone.)

MADELINE. Prick! He beat me to it! *(She slams down the phone.)* Next time I'm going to hang up on you when I say I will!

PETE. *(Talking to his genitals.)* I rented this movie for YOU! And I'm not renting any more unless you can stay awake and watch them.

(End of Scene)

(MADELINE is dressed nicely and wearing sock puppets on her hands. One of the puppets has hair made from zippers. She speaks to an audience.)

MADELINE. Okay, shall we—all right shall we—come on, shall we—let's let's let's—everybody, come on, come on—

shall we—let's come on—NO, no no no nonononononononono—
Kaiesha, Emma—watch that over there—that's a bad desk,
bad desk, bad—don't sit—Jaime, move the desk, so no one—
Julian, there's water—that's the bad water place—they'll fix
that someday, but now we have to—Dorcas and Cloud, sit on
the right—Shona and Tyrone, move away from the window—
the screen isn't really—yes, just come here now, now now
now NOW. All right. Time for Madeline and Zipper Man.

    ZIPPER MAN *(Puppet.)* Whoa, Madeline, I got some phat
rhymes today.

    MADELINE. *(Puppet.)* Who you calling fat, Zip?

    ZIPPER MAN *(Puppet.)* No, Madeline. I'm not dissing you.
These rhymes are dope. They from an old grandmama called
Mother Goose.

    MADELINE. *(Puppet.)* Well, lay them down upon us.

(ZIPPER MAN raps the rhyme while MADELINE bops to it.)

    ZIPPER MAN *(Puppet.)*
Humpty Dumpty sat on a wall,
Humpty Dumpty had a great fall,
All the king's horses
All the king's men
Couldn't put Humpty together again.

    MADELINE. *(Puppet.)* Oh man, poor Humpty dude. *(Answering a question, back to her own voice.)* What? No, Humpty
just fell, Rosita—I'm sure he wasn't pushed. Tawanda? No, he
wasn't shot either. He just fell off the wall. Kevin? No, they
didn't have snipers in those days and they didn't have cars to
drive by in. Sunil? No, honey, they didn't have police, either.
All the king's men were the police, and they tried to put him

together—they really, really tried—they didn't just leave him there.

MADELINE *(Puppet.)* Yo, Zip! This Mother Goose got some more rhymes?

ZIPPER MAN *(Puppet.)*
Goosey, goosey, gander,
Whither does thou wander?
Upstairs and downstairs
And in my lady's chamber.

There I met an old man
Who would not say his prayers;
I took him by the left leg,
And threw him down the stairs.

MADELINE *(Puppet.)* You all like that one better! Madeline can tell!

MADELINE *(Person.)* Hiroko? Why are you crying, honey? It's only a—She did? Well, honey, I'm sure she didn't mean to hurt him, and I'm sorry you had to see that. No, Mother Goose doesn't live in your building. This was written a long time ago, in another country. Madeline and Zipper Man are out of rhymes for today, so this is the end of the library period. Line up and meet your teacher in the hall. Bye-bye.

MADELINE *(Puppet.)* Bye.
ZIPPER MAN *(Puppet.)* Bye.
MADELINE. *(Puppet.)* Bye.
ZIPPER MAN *(Puppet.)* Bye.
MADELINE. *(Person.)* Bye.

(DAVID enters—a young male teacher with glasses.)

DAVID. Madeline.

MADELINE. David. Big bomb.

DAVID. Not you, baby. *(To someone offstage.)* Here she is, Ted! She's all mine now. *(He kisses her neck and feels her up.)* You look beautiful in puppets. You coming to the faculty meeting? I'll pick you up.

MADELINE. I'll need picking up by then.

DAVID. I'm your man. *(Kisses her on the earlobe.)* Bye.

(He exits. MADELINE waves bye with one of her puppets because it's still on her hand. She notices the puppet, it attacks her throat, the other puppet pulls it off. MADELINE crosses to a pay telephone, takes puppets off, puts in a quarter, dials. PETE picks up.)

MADELINE. Is it sexual harassment when you want them to do it?

PETE. Oh, Maddy.

MADELINE. But they only do it in public, in front of other people, when you've got puppets on your hands?

PETE. Are you still at school?

MADELINE. Couldn't wait. And has it ever occurred to you how violent Mother Goose is? It's one little horror story after another.

PETE. What's left?

MADELINE. I tried Anansi the spider—they're afraid of bugs. Any story with rodents of any kind is definitely out. I'm looking for a fable involving a lost piece of asphalt looking for its pot hole or the story of the brave little R train that thought it could huff and puff its way to Connecticut.

PETE. So what are you cooking for the showdown with

David the neckkisser?

MADELINE. Some chicken thing with lots of wine. Or maybe we'll go to that Bojar place by the entrance to the Six?

PETE. More alone time—the better. Call me.

MADELINE. Nothing's going to happen, Peter.

PETE. You don't know that.

MADELINE. That man is a classic clit tease. He's all over me in public, in front of our friends. As soon as I get him alone, he won't touch me.

PETE. Use a condom.

MADELINE. For what? Party favors? Water balloons? Shall we blow them up and let them fly around the room?

PETE. Think positively.

MADELINE. I want him, Pete. It's been like this for months. He's got me almost obsessed and we've never been alone.

PETE. Cook that chicken. Buy those condoms

(PETE and MADELINE hang up.)

MADELINE. Even clit teases have to eat. *(Pause.)* Hope is lemon chicken with no garlic.

(MADELINE exits. BERNICE is lying on the floor. Her walker is nowhere to be seen.)

BERNICE. I've sifted through my life and I can't find a single reason why I should be lying here on my own bathroom floor while my sister Bea is happily married for the third time in San Diego. But, you know, I bet anything, I bet you fifty dollars that she will be nursing him in six months and spending her hard-earned dollars on a hefty nurse to lift him in and out of the bathtub. Men are such weaklings. How they got control of the world I don't know. It's because women have no guts and are afraid to make anybody mad because they hate to be alone. And how do most of them end up? Alone! Ow. Ow. 'Course what do I know, I'm lying on my own bathroom floor. Don't you know that when they find me, some young prick is gonna say, "She's fallen and she can't get up." Oh, the young. I'm so jealous of them. The beautiful are cruel and stupid—there's no doubt about it. I'm glad I went to the mall and got a decent bathroom rug the last time. Bathrooms always remind me of confessionals. Not that our confessional was ever tiled. But I did feel sitting in there with the priest like we were on a two-holer—a kind of really nice one with walls to separate the sexes and a little grate to talk through, like they might of had in Venice. Although I suspect most people just went in the canals. Oh, we're a dirty bird, mankind. Dirty, dirty— *(Sees something.)* —I've got to tell Henreeka to do a better job on this floor, particularly around this bathtub. It's strange I'm not in more pain. Maybe I've had a stroke. Oh god, I'll be a vegetable! Wait a minute—I'm talking. Vegetables don't talk, old girl. I'm dead. I just *think* I'm talking, and I'm actually—HELLLLLP! HELLLLLLLLLLP! HELLLLLLPPP! *(She whistles.)* There's an echo. The dead don't make echoes. HELLLLLLP GODDAMITT!!! MADELINNNNNNNNNNE!!!

(End of Scene)

(JACKIE has his back to the audience—he's putting some cream on his face.)

JACKIE. Ow. Just a sec— *(He turns around and we see that he has a black eye and facial contusions. He's looking in the mirror, putting on make-up.)* I normally hate make-up. This is pimple cover-up. I don't think Clearasil ever imagined the uses it would be put to. This shit happens. Not from fag bashers—I'd be face-down in the river, floating out to sea. This shit happens from my dates now and again. This one was an accountant—goes to show you never know people. If the guy hitting you is gay it's not fag bashing. Right? I'll be all right. It's a lot worse than it looks. Reverse that.

(End of Scene)

(MADELINE is sitting with a glass of wine—she is eating the remains of something from a pot. Phone rings—she picks up.)

PETE. Pretend I'm selling something and hang up on me if anything—

MADELINE. Hello, Peter.

PETE. No, really—just pretend—I—I—had to know, so—

MADELINE. I'm alone, Peter.

PETE. Oh.

MADELINE. But the chicken was good. We talked about it endlessly.

PETE. Oh god.

MADELINE. And the apartment. Loves my apartment. Has lots of personality—like me. I think personality in the female must be like salt peter in the meat.

PETE. Maybe he's a closet case.

MADELINE. No, maybe I am. Maybe I'm a Lesbian. Maybe I give off Lesbian vibes that only men pick up. Like those whistles that only dogs can hear.

PETE. Do you have sexual fantasies about women?

MADELINE. No. But maybe it's so buried, Peter, that— wait a minute, I did have a crush on my Girl Scout counselor when I was eleven or so—

PETE. I don't know, Madeline. I knew when I was five or six.

MADELINE. Yeah, but you've always been precocious.

PETE. Yeah, Pete Szczepanek, the sexual prodigy. Burned out before he could get free of the nuns. And what good has it done me? I'm getting fucking desperate here. I'm about to encase myself in latex and go to the park. I need some infusion of...something. Slease may be the answer.

MADELINE. Be careful.

PETE. Rough trade.

MADELINE. Be careful.

PETE. Shut up!

MADELINE. I'm just—

PETE. I know.

MADELINE. Uh-oh—let me take this call. Maybe he's changed his mind.

PETE. Take it. Bye.

(PETE hangs up.)

MADELINE. *(Still on phone.)* Yes? This is her daughter. What?! Is she all right?! Oh my god. Oh my god.

(End of Scene)

(Sound of an irritatingly cheerful song from the late Forties or early Fifties, as sung by Jo Stafford or Kay Ballard, comes from a small transistor radio on BERNICE'S chairside table—the song repeats and repeats, in what seems to be an infinite loop, stuck on the chorus. MADELINE and BERNICE are in BERNICE'S apartment and MADELINE'S boredom borders on the supernatural. BERNICE has her feet up and is wearing a brace on one leg. They stare. BERNICE turns off radio—she sees something out of the window. It's a plastic bag flying around.)

BERNICE. Look at that! That's the same plastic bag that was flying around up here three hours ago!

MADELINE. YOU MEAN, BEFORE (name of song) STARTED TO PLAY?

BERNICE. No, I'm serious. Isn't that something?

MADELINE. IT'S NOT THE SAME BAG.

BERNICE. Yes, it is.

MADELINE. NO, IT'S NOT!

BERNICE. Dammit, MADELINE—I think I know my plastic bags when I see them.

MADELINE. IS IT YOUR PERSONAL PLASTIC BAG? HMMMMMMM?

BERNICE. It goddam is if it's flying around outside my balcony!

MADELINE. THAT PLASTIC YOU SAW OUTSIDE WAS FROM DUANE READE! THIS PLASTIC BAG IS FROM A&S! AND THAT BALCONY IS NOT A BALCONY! IT IS A HIGH-DIVING BOARD FOR SUICIDES!!!!

BERNICE. You need to get out more. You need a boyfriend that's not a homo.

MADELINE. Pete is not my boyfriend, Mother. For Chrissake.

BERNICE. Well, you know that. And I know that. And Pete knows that. The rest of the world—I dunno.

MADELINE. TO HELL WITH THE REST OF THE WORLD.

BERNICE. You've got a bad attitude. You've stopped trying. I mean, look at your hair. What is that?

MADELINE. MOTHER, THE DYNEL WIG LOOK AND BIG HAIR WENT OUT DECADES AGO!

BERNICE. If Oprah can lose a hundred pounds, why can't you? And Tom Arnold lost a hundred and even that ex-wife of his lost some, too.

MADELINE. HER NAME IS ROSEANNE, MOTHER.

BERNICE. Well, whatever.

MADELINE. Her name is ROSEANNE, MOTHER. ROSEANNE, ROSEANNE, ROSEANNE!!!!

BERNICE. Are you a Lesbian, honey? Because you could tell me if you were. And if you are, and I'm NOT saying you are. But IF you are, I'd think you'd be attracted to someone more, well, attractive, like Cindy Crawford girl or that girl on "Cheers" who cries all the time. Now those are nice-looking women. No, Tom Arnold's ex-wife just can't take off that weight. Born fat. Died fat. Her curse. Hmmp. What were we talking about?

MADELINE. LIZZIE BORDEN.

BERNICE. Is she the one with the weight program where you buy the food?

MADELINE. NO, THAT IS JENNY CRAIG!

BERNICE. Well, what about that? Have you tried that? The food comes in plastic bags—*there* it is! See? That's my plastic bag! Now what does it say on it?

MADELINE. MACY'S.

BERNICE. Huh. So that's what we've come to. A fine store like Macy's floating by on a plastic bag. That's your world, honey. So much trash in the sky. I'm sorry. Well, let's see what's on the radio. *(MADELINE takes the radio and throws it off the balcony. BERNICE quietly turns on the lamp—it plays the same irritatingly cheerful song. MADELINE throws the lamp off the balcony. BERNICE picks up a ballpoint pen and clicks it—the same irritatingly cheerful song comes out of it. MADELINE takes the pen and stamps on it.)* Well, lets watch tv. Maybe Lawrence Welk is on.

(BERNICE clicks the remote. We see Lawrence Welk.)

LAWRENCE WELK. Anda now for dat wunnerful song of love, (name of song) A-one, a-two, a-tree—

(Chorus of the song takes over. BERNICE is so pleased.)

MADELINE. Vodka still in the cupboard?
LAWRENCE WELK. *(To MADELINE.)* Helpa yourself.

(MADELINE exits to get the vodka. Light change. The television is on to white noise. MADELINE is drunk and dialing the phone. BERNICE is asleep in front of the television.)

MADELINE. Be home. Be home. Be home.

(It rings in PETE'S apartment. Finally, the answering machine comes on.)

PETE'S RECORDED VOICE. You have reached the answering machine of Pete Szczepanek. The poetry selection today is from Hart Crane:
"There are no stars tonight
But those of memory
Yet how much room for memory there is
In the loose girdle of soft rain."
We love you, Hart. Don't jump.

(Sound of the beep. MADELINE just hangs up the phone. She gets up and turns off the television and helps BERNICE up from the chair.)

MADELINE. Come on, Mom. Come on. Here's your walker. We'll stop at the potty.
BERNICE. I do not pee in a potty.
MADELINE. Toilet. Come on.
BERNICE. Don't ever call it that.
MADELINE. Yes, Mom.

(MADELINE and BERNICE exit.)

(End of Scene)

(PETE is sitting in his bathrobe, watching television. He flicks between channels, absently, getting the usual snippets.)

PETE. And then he went to the bar. *(More channel surfing.)* And then he got up and got dressed and went to the bar.

He went to the bar and he had a nice time. And he met someone. And they went to get something to eat. And it was good. And then... and then... they went to the guy's apartment. And it was a really nice apartment—no, we don't care about the apartment. Fuck the apartment. The guy kissed him in the elevator. And *then* they went into the apartment. And they... didn't have sex yet, they just talked. And they each had a popper—no, they didn't do that—they haven't done that in years! *(Rattles his head.)* Boy, these are really old files. No, let's see—they talked and talked until there was only silence left and they knew. And Pete didn't have to do anything. The guy just took him because he couldn't wait any more. And he said things under his breath that Pete couldn't quite understand and Pete got very, very hot and... and... *(About the heat in the apartment.)* It's hot in here. Ech. *(Sounds of a commercial sex ad, from Channel 35.)* Lesbian sex for straight men on the commercial sex channel. *(Switches channels.)* And what are the homos doing on Channel 69? They're singing show tunes! *(PETE starts to sing along, softly at first, then tries to get into the song.)* Oh my god. Oh my god, this is pathetic. I don't even like this music. *(He picks up the phone and pushes the speed dial.)*

MADELINE'S V.O. Fabio and I are out walking the guard dogs, so leave a message.

PETE *(Into the phone.)* My message is: AHHHHHHHHHHH. AHHHHHHHHHH. AHHH. *(Normal voice.)* I'm going to bed.

(PETE clicks off and exits.)

(End of Scene)

*(MADELINE is a little drunk and in a church, talking to a
statue of the Virgin.)*

MADELINE. I know we haven't had a good relationship
since that time in high school when, I felt, you really let me
down. I guess I let you down, too. I just expected you to understand since you had been in the same position. I waited in
the backyard all night, on the terrace, and you never came, I
never got a single feeling, no message, nothing—just the big
cosmos, surrounded by a circle of orange from the lights off
the avenue, just all that black sky with those holes of light
staring back at me. I begin to feel like Sereta Lopez was right,
that we were all just bugs inside a really big coffee can with a
black plastic lid that some little mean white boy was keeping
and he poked holes in the lid just to let us breathe a little and
those holes let in light and we thought they were stars. So I
had the abortion, Mary, and I never needed to use birth control again. And Pete was the one who drove me there and back
and talked to me while I lay in the backseat with a towel between my legs because fucking Ray—that's what we always
called him after that—that was his generic name because that
pretty much defined him—Fucking Ray wanted nothing to do
with it since he was ashamed of knocking up a fat girl. And it
was Pete who got me back into the house and sat up and drank
with my mother who thought I was just broken-hearted over
some guy which I was, but I was also mourning my womb
which was pretty much a goner, too. And after that, Ray's
Camarro had its headlights busted out about six times a year
by an unknown vandal in various locations around the city
until Fucking Ray got married and moved to Sparta. And Pete
stopped carrying a hammer in his bookbag. As you can tell,

I'm still pissed that I never heard from you. You would not believe the world, Blessed Mother. And from whatever place you see it—those mountaintops in Yugoslavia, which doesn't exist anymore, by the way—from those tacos and potato chips and tree trunks that people see you in—from wherever— you must have noticed how really like the Last Days it is. So I'm just here to let bygones be bygones, and to ask you to please protect Peter. I forgive you, by the way, wherever you are. *(Looking up at the heavens.)* For godssake, I know this is just a bunch of plaster here.

(MADELINE crosses herself and exits.)

(End of Scene)

(PETE is outside, trying to cruise. He crosses the stage and exits. After a beat, he crosses back, slowly, trying to watch someone. He stops and tries to look sexy. A MAN enters, crosses to him.)

MAN. Hi.

PETE. What? Oh! Yes! Hello! I was passing. I live—I live near here, and I was just—. ... I always thought it was so ador- able—"Gay Street." Have to live there. I wonder who...? Lucky people, whoever. What a name! What's in a name? Yeah.

(MAN exits.)

PETE. *(To the now absent MAN.)* It's the Prozac. I left my other personality at home. *(To himself.)* Oh yeah, I'm a funny, funny man.

(PETE starts to exit one way, then changes his mind, then changes it again and exits.)

(End of Scene)

MADELINE V.O. Madeline's Dating Life: A Puppet Play.

(Lights up on two sock puppets—MADELINE puppet and a MAN puppet. The MADELINE puppet plays all the WOMAN parts.)

WOMAN. I really enjoyed dinner tonight.

MAN. That was a nice little place.

WOMAN. Yes, it was nice. Do you want to come in for a cup of something?

MAN. Sure.

(PUPPETS mime entering the "apartment.")

MAN. Nice apartment.

WOMAN. Thanks.

MAN. Come sit next to me on the sofa.

WOMAN. Sure.

(PUPPETS try to fake sitting.)

MAN. We've been going out for a while now.

WOMAN. A month. And I've really enjoyed it.

MAN. Maddy. You're a very nice woman. But I just don't feel...that way about you. I've been trying to get over a bad relationship and I just can't... What I really need is a friend, not a lover.

WOMAN. Fine.

MAN. I hope you're not upset.

WOMAN. No.

MAN. I just don't feel...

WOMAN. Fine.

MAN. ... that way about you.

WOMAN. Fine.

MAN. I hope we can be—

WOMAN. Fine.

MAN. Let me tell you my entire life story.

WOMAN. Fine.

(PUPPETS hold, then disappear, as puppets do. Lights remain on the "Puppet stage".)

MADELINE V.O. Act Two.

(Two sock puppets—MAN and WOMAN appear. This time the MAN is different.)

WOMAN. I really enjoyed dinner tonight.

MAN. That was a nice little place.

WOMAN. Yes, it was nice. Do you want to come in for a cup of something?

MAN. Sure. *(PUPPETS enter.)* I feel so close to you, Maddy.

(He snuggles WOMAN close to him.)

WOMAN. I'm glad.

MAN. I can really talk to you.

WOMAN. That's nice. I can talk to you, too.

MAN. I'm so in love with your friend, Irene. Oh, Maddy, can you talk to her for me?

WOMAN. I'd rather shoot myself in the foot, thank you.

MAN. What?

WOMAN. I'll try, Jerry. Don't you want some ice cream???

(PUPPETS disappear.)

MADELINE V.O. Act Seven.

(Two sock puppets appear—MAN and WOMAN. MAN is different again.)

MAN. I really enjoyed dinner tonight. The chicken—

WOMAN. —was good, yes. You said.

MAN. Cute apartment—lots of—

WOMAN. —personality—thanks.

MAN. This upholstery—

WOMAN. Fine.

MAN. Woodwork—

WOMAN. Fine.

MAN. I just don't feel...

WOMAN. Fine.

MAN. ... that way about you.

WOMAN. Fine.

MAN. I hope we can be—

WOMAN. Sign the book. It's in alphabetical order.

MADELINE V.O. Act Four Hundred and Thirty-Two.

(Two sock puppets appear—MAN and WOMAN. They are snuggling.)

MAN. I feel so close to you, Maddy. *(MAN snuggles closer to her.)* I could sit like this for hours. But I've got a date with this humpy German boy I met at the bar. *(WOMAN disappears.)* Madeline? Didn't I tell you I was gay? *(WOMAN pops up holding a can of International Coffee in her mouth.)* Vienna Mocha?

(MAN and WOMAN cheer in delight and exit.)

MADELINE V.O. The mini-series.

WOMAN. I really enjoyed dinner tonight.

MAN. That was a nice little place.

WOMAN. Yes, it was nice. Do you want to come in for a cup of something?

MAN. Sure. *(PUPPETS mime entering the "apartment".)* Nice apartment.

WOMAN. Thanks.

MAN. Come sit next to me on the sofa.

WOMAN. Sure.

(PUPPETS try to fake sitting.)

MAN. We've been going out for a while now.

WOMAN. A month. And I've really enjoyed it.

MAN. Madeline, you're a wonderful woman. I just don't feel that way about you. But I value our friendship so much...

(WOMAN PUPPET devours MAN PUPPET, making terrible

noises, pulling PUPPET off hand—with her mouth—and tossing it away.)

WOMAN. *(Satisfied.)* Haaaaa.

(PUPPETS disappear.)

(End of Scene)

(JACKIE and PETE are together at a hotel.)

JACKIE. This is a nice hotel. *(Pause.)* You seem nervous again. Sure you don't have a wife or a lover that's going to knock on that door?

PETE. Yes. I'm sure.

JACKIE. Maybe they're going to call?

PETE. No. No one's going to call. OR come through that door. Or any door that I'm on the other side of.

JACKIE. You've never been to a whore. Before now, huh?

PETE. I don't go to whores. I'm gay.

JACKIE. I meant gay whores.

PETE You mean hustlers.

JACKIE. Now you're getting on some word power trip thing with me. How did this happen?

PETE. You're a hustler.

JACKIE. I call myself a whore.

PETE. That's a girl's name.

JACKIE. Mary, what's wrong?

PETE. "Mary?" You're too young to remember that.

JACKIE. So? It' can't be mine?

PETE. We don't do that any more.

JACKIE. Who decided that? It must've been in that newsletter I didn't get because I don't have an address.

PETE. We never use those names. We're men.

JACKIE. Well, I'm not a hustler. I don't try that hard. I don't hustle anything and I don't do that stupid dance from the seventies. I'm a whore. It's an old and noble profession.

PETE. I'm sorry. I don't know what I'm doing. Politics. Help.

JACKIE. Can I ask you something?

PETE. Sure.

JACKIE. Something personal?

PETE. More personal than my winkie?

JACKIE. Cocks aren't personal. Eyes are. *(Pause.)* In the old days, you know. In the days before, you know—

PETE. AIDS.

JACKIE. Condoms. Was it really great to take a man's naked cock in your mouth and have him thrust or whatever and not worry about the condom breaking and then when he came, you could taste him and just lie back and not throw anything away?

(Beat.)

PETE. Yeah. It was really wonderful. The head's very soft, you know. And it feels good... against... your... tongue.

(Beat.)'

JACKIE. I thought so.

PETE.. And you get all sticky with that clean smell of cum.

JACKIE. How does it taste?

PETE. You mean you never...?

JACKIE. How old were you when you sucked you first cock?

PETE. Fourteen. 1968. Boy Scout Camp. Aptly named.

JACKIE. Why? Nevermind. When did you first start using condoms?

PETE. Six years ago.

JACKIE. Six years ago, I was—eleven. I saw this program about the Greeks. They did what they wanted. And they put it on pottery, too. It was a golden age.

PETE. You're 17?!

JACKIE. No, twenty. I was exaggerating.

PETE. Twenty?!

JACKIE. All right—twenty-one!! What are you worried about, anyway?! Like, they're going to bust you for me being jail-bait? We're both jail-bait! We're queer!!

PETE. Oh man.

JACKIE. Listen, we don't have to do anything. There's this series on the Bible that I like where this fat British fruit takes you all over the Holy Land and tells you where the stories really came from. I mean, you paid for the room. Don't make me leave. I'll be quiet. Okay? Okay, Paul.

PETE. My name's Pete.

JACKIE. Okay, Pete?

PETE. Come here.

JACKIE. With or without music?

PETE. Just come here.

JACKIE. I usually don't get too close...

PETE. Me, either.

JACKIE. I'm a little scared. Actually.

PETE. Me, too. Come here. Mary.

JACKIE. I'm Jackie.
PETE. Jackie. Jack. *(Whispers.)* Jack.

(JACKIE goes to PETE—they kiss.)

(END OF ACT ONE)

ACT II

(Lights up on MADELINE'S apartment. She is recycling. It is after PETE'S birthday dinner at Zen Palate. CHARLIE is there, still dressed well.)

MADELINE. Charlie, why are you here?

CHARLIE. The downstairs door was propped open.

MADELINE. You didn't shut it, did you? Mr. Rodriguez is carrying out all his newspapers.

CHARLIE. No. It took a couple of years off my life, but I left it open. He is gonna shut it, isn't he?

MADELINE. No, he likes to leave it open, so that all the murderers and rapists can come in because they're all members of his family, not being Irish or Polish—the "good" people!

CHARLIE. Oh, Madeline, come on—I'm not that bad. I just will not let myself be fleeced by some rich Japanese Person—

MADELINE. Oh, "Japanese person"? Is that what it is now?

CHARLIE. No one in that restaurant heard it.

MADELINE. I did.

CHARLIE. Madeline, I ask you—thirty bucks for that egg roll and that tiny little piece of bait?!!

MADELINE. It's a vegetarian restaurant—that wasn't "bait", I mean, fish—it was bean curd or something.

CHARLIE. Beans aren't supposed to have curd, in my opinion. Is that was I was *eating?* Jesus Christ!

MADELINE. And it was twenty bucks because you ordered two entrees.

57

CHARLIE. I need to eat. Look at me.

MADELINE. Charlie, I left the restaurant because you pissed me off!

CHARLIE. I know.

MADELINE. You always piss me off. Why do you *do* that?

CHARLIE. I know. *(Pause.)* Look. Madeline. I've accepted my son's sexuality. I can deal with young Black men calling me "cracker" and "honky" and "pig" and not blow, like some of my fellow... police persons. I can help defend abortion clinics because of the way I feel about rights and my job as a cop, even though you KNOW how I feel about abortion—

MADELINE. Yeah, that was New Years. As I recall, we cleared the Chelsea Trattoria with that little discussion.

CHARLIE. Now, that was a good meal. Anyway, I can deal with all sorts of immigrants who don't speak English or wish to when MY grandparents went to goddam night school to learn!

MADELINE. Where are the damn ties?

CHARLIE. I just want some acknowledgement of how far I've come and had to come!

MADELINE. Charlie, you've lived in New York your whole life. Why do you get so angry?

CHARLIE. Because I've lived in New York my whole life! And you know I put up with much more than you and Peter. I'm on the streets, Zelda! And your generation—I'm sick to death of hearing about it. What about MY generation? Before we even got to your goddam part of this

this century, we had plenty of our own tragedies! The Depression, the War—a *world* war—and gangsters, not gangstas, like every two-bit rap song says.

MADELINE. Listen to a lot of rap down there in the station?

CHARLIE. There? Every—goddam—where!! It's shoved down my throat in this godforsaken city. Bass beats shaking the whole goddam block. Some Nissan sentra with tinted windows rolling by, pounding out some beat that sounds like cannon fire. I *swear* I wish it was cannon fire sometimes, so I could reply in kind! AND I KNOW YOU'RE JUST WAITING FOR ME TO SAY IT!!!

MADELINE. What, Charlie?

CHARLIE. That word. You know.

MADELINE. No, I don't know.

CHARLIE. You're just trying to make me say it.

MADELINE. "Gook?" Faggot?"

CHARLIE. No, the "*N* word"!!

MADELINE. Oh, yeah—"*n*o progress", "*n*o hope", "*n*o future", "*N*armageddon!!"

CHARLIE. DON'T BLAME ME FOR THIS WORLD! I fought in World War II and now I'm fighting Street War III!

MADELINE. Wait a minute, wait a minute. You were in Korea.

CHARLIE. Whatever! The point is I'm still protecting Koreans, and Japanese, and Indonesians and Australians—

MADELINE. Australians? Australians don't need protecting.

CHARLIE. If they're in New York City, they do!!

MADELINE. Well, fine, Mr. Protector! Come to my school sometime and convince my kids they're being protected— alright? Convince LaWanda and Carlos and Ping and Fiona and Hiroko who saw a man thrown down her stairs by one of your police persons! The child can't make it through a simple nursery rhyme without crying!

CHARLIE. Well, that's not my fault!

MADELINE. Well, it's not my fault, either!

CHARLIE. Madeline, if I knew how to fix it, I'd fix it! There was a time when you thought I could do anything.

MADELINE. I was fifteen. My mother was insane. You were my favorite person.

CHARLIE. How is Bernice?

MADELINE. Fine. She loved the fruit. *(About the garbage bags.)* Where are the LONGER TIES THAT ACTUALLY HOLD THE BAGS SHUT????

CHARLIE. You don't need them. Here. You just use the top of the bag. *(He ties the top for her.)* See?

MADELINE. Thanks.

CHARLIE. So I'm taking Pete on a vacation. And not one of those stupid tours. I planned it myself—I got a deal for late May.

MADELINE. That's really nice. I mean that.

CHARLIE. You don't want to go, do you?

MADELINE. I can't. I'm socked in until June. *(Beat.)* You're relieved, aren't you?

CHARLIE. *(Really disappointed.)* No. No, Maddy, I'm not.

MADELINE. I thought you knew when my school—

CHARLIE. I guess I forgot. I'll take this bag down— *(He exits, re-enters.)* Do you know the door to the street is still wide open down there?

MADELINE. It takes time for him to get everything out.

He's old.

CHARLIE. Like me.

MADELINE. I'm not taking that bait. Okay?

CHARLIE. You're a tough cookie. I'm going home. *(MADELINE crosses to him and kisses him on the cheek. CHARLIE strokes her cheek.)* 'Bye, Zelda.

(CHARLIE exits with the newspapers.)

MADELINE. Bye. Thanks. Watch it— Bye.

(CHARLIE'S gone. MADELINE touches the place on her cheek where CHARLIE touched her, looks confused, then dials PETE, gets his answering machine.)

PETE V.O. You're reached Pete's machine. It's such a burden being clever. Leave a message.

MADELINE. Peter. This is Madeline. You know that older man who lived with your mother and claimed to be your father? He was just here. What is *with* him lately?

(MADELINE hangs up.)

(End of Scene)

(JACKIE is sitting in Central Park.)

JACKIE. It's my favorite time of day—4:30 a.m. or so or maybe it's five—not night, not morning. The city is, like, sleeping really badly, the kind of sleep where, it it's a person sleeping, they make noises? Sometimes they say your name, if they know it, if you *told* them. Sometimes they say someone else's name. Sometimes they holler, like from a bad dream, but they don't wake up. This is the only time of day I ever really think about... going home. Well, there was that really bad week last winter, but you know, you know, they don't say it, but they think they're better than you are. They do. They think they know things. How To Live. How To Not be On The Street. And A Eyesore and A Pain in The Ass of Society. It's one big talk show and you're the poor white trash guest with the stupid hair-do and the really bad jeans screaming at your husband who's really your cousin or something. And one half of the room wants to kill you and the other half wants to save you. I have to say I've seen more of the ones who want to save you. I guess I'm lucky. I'm here. But even that saving thing— you can see it in their eyes—it's fucking scary. It's some warped, fucked-up version of love at first sight. You're their little "Help Baby." And that look, that look. *(He shakes off the look.)* So whether it's a nun or a trick, either one, I take something of theirs— *(JACKIE shows PETE'S ring on his finger)* —so when they wake up the next morning, they feel ripped off so we're equals. I come here because you can see the sky better, so it's really night when it's night. They say you can see the Park from the air—way out in space. I try to be quiet because, you know, a person could get hurt here— because it is dark and very secluded. I hope. (He hears a shout.) That's nothing to be scared about—New York City'll wake up soon and have some pancakes, and everything will be... fine. *(One bird chirp.)* The sun's not even up and they start to sing to it. How do they know that the sun's gonna come up? Ever heard of a "bird-brain"? They're not a smart animal. But they know it somehow. *(Suddenly, the air is filled with bird chirpings.)* And it's still daaaaark!

(JACKIE stands and lifts his arms like an orchestra conductor—the chirpings build to a great crescendo—he reaches to the sky with the sound.)

(End of Scene)

(At a bar. PETE walks in, carrying his briefcase. He's come from a meeting.)

BRAD. *(Very fey bar waiter.)* Hello.
PETE. Where's the piano bar?
BRAD. We sold it.

(RUBY crosses to BRAD. He's an older transvestite, played by MOTHER, wearing a cowboy hat and carrying another.)

RUBY. Brad.
BRAD. No.
RUBY. Brad.
BRAD. I hate the fucking thing and I fucking won't wear it! All right? *(RUBY just stands there, offering the hat.)* We're in New York, not Wyoming, Ruby! I came to New York City to live in New York City! If I'd wanted to wear cowboy hats, I would have stayed at home!!
PETE. Where are you from?
BRAD. Indiana.
PETE. Do they wear cowboy hats in Indiana?

BRAD. Psychologically, yes.

PETE. Hello, Ruby.

RUBY. Hello, Peter.

PETE. Is that a new wig?

RUBY. Yes, it's fabulous, isn't it? My mother bought it for me. *(Takes off her cowboy hat.)* See? No hat hair. It bounces right back. *(About his breasts.)* And look at these. I went back to falsies. I'm not doing the surgery, I stopped taking the hormones, I'm shaving, I'm a man, I have a dick—deal with it. I think it's the cowboy hat. Right, Brad?

PETE. *(To BRAD.)* Is this a country-western night or something?

BRAD. Oh, you poor darling, you don't know, do you?

RUBY. *(Offering hat.)* Brad?

BRAD. NO! GODDAMMIT!!

RUBY *(Exiting.)* Mr. Joondee won't like it.

BRAD. *(Under his breath.)* I don't give a fuck what Mr. fucking Joondee fucking likes! *(To PETE.)* Peter, what's happening to the world? I came to New York to be a faggot, not a cowboy! And what is Ruby doing in a cowboy hat? He's been wearing his mother's clothes since he was eight! They started shopping together when he was fourteen! He's worked his whole life to turn himself into a elegantly-dressed woman! And now this!!

PETE. What happened?

BRAD. The Morocco has become a fucking country western bar!! Queer bars have to have concepts to compete! Didn't you know? It's not enough to have a nice, relatively clean place with a piano bar, tufted stools and a lighted disco floor. Noooo! All the theatre posters? Kiss them good-bye! Judy? Marilyn? Bette Davis? Even that old Laurette Taylor billboard? Bye,

bye! And what's worse is that our concept is passé but Mr. Joondee doesn't know that because he's still living in the fucking Seventies!

PETE. But it still says "Morocco." And the tables and everything—

BRAD. It's all gonna go. *(Sits.)* I've got to sit down. *(About the decor to come.)* Okay. Striped pine furniture. Knotty pine panelling. Ever seen knotty pine? Lots of little eyes looking at you, all over the wall. Saw dust on the floor. Barrels here and there. Bales of hay? I mean, back to the barn, darling. It's gonna look like a bad prom in Bumfuck, Oklahoma! I wouldn't be surprised if Mr. Fucking Joondee doesn't send us a carton of cow patties that we can fling here and there for some of that *real* country feeling! I swear I'm going to go work at Splash— at least it'll be clean!

RUBY. *(Offstage.)* Brad!

(RUBY throws him the cowboy hat. BRAD picks it up and puts it on his head, stands up, defeated.)

BRAD. *(The speech Mr. Joondee wants him to say to each customer.)* Howdy. Cow. Poke. What would you all like to drink?

PETE. I'd like a white wine, please.

BRAD. *(Tearful gratitude.)* Thank God for you, Peter!!

(BRAD exits. TIM enters, dressed in a cowboy hat, looking very cowboy.)

TIM. Howdy.

PETE. Someone already took my order.

TIM. *(Really coming on.)* Did they? What did you order?
PETE. Beer.
TIM. Can I sit down?
PETE. *(Voice getting too high.)* Yes. *(Correcting.)* Yeah.
TIM. *(Sitting.)* So, you like cowboys?
PETE. Maybe.
BRAD. *(Enters with two drinks.)* Here's your white wine. *(To TIM.)* And your Perrier with a twist. *(Country-western music starts.)* It's the end of civilization as we know it, darlings.

(BRAD exits.)

TIM. Ever done the Texas Two-Step?
PETE. I don't know. Is it hard?
TIM. We'll just have to find that out, won't we?

(TIM takes PETE by the hand and lifts him out of the chair, pulls him to him, shows him where the hands go for the dance.)

PETE. Are you a real cowboy?
TIM. Under our clothes, we're all the same.
PETE. And some of us are even better than that.
TIM. There you go. You're getting it.

(TIM dances with PETE. Light and music change—they are in PETER'S apartment, having had sex right inside the door, on the rug. PETER is stunned and happy.)

TIM. *(Cowboy persona gone.)* That was fabulous. It's better on the floor. Nice apartment. I think you left your keys in the door. Hey, that rhymed. Speak to me.

PETE. Things are good. I'm back.

TIM. Back from where?

PETE. The desert.

TIM. The desert?

PETE. It's just been a while.

TIM. You seemed pent up. Why don't we get up off the floor?

PETE. Right.

TIM. Where's the loo? I'll take the condoms.

(TIM kisses PETE as he takes his condom off.)

PETE. It's right through there.

(TIM gets up and exits to the john.)

PETE. Oh my god. I'm happy.

(PETE gets up and goes to the phone, starts to pick it up, thinks. TIM re-enters.)

TIM. Can't get it to flush. Who are you calling? Boy, you're over me quick.

PETE. No! I was just calling. Do you want to stay the night?

TIM. You were calling to cancel someone.

PETE. No. I have no one to cancel.

TIM. *(A joke.)* Do you know what Lesbians do on the second date?

PETE. No.

TIM. Move in together. Do you know what gay men do on the second date?

PETE. No.

TIM. Stop having sex. That won't be us, will it?

PETE. No way.

TIM. Okay—prove it. The second date starts right now.

PETE. Come on.

TIM. This is such a nice apartment. I have Lesbian tendencies, you know.

PETE. Come on, cowboy.

(They exit to the bedroom. Phone rings.)

PETE'S VOICE. *(On answering machine.)* You have reached 555-4320. No poetry today. Leave message after beep. Bye.

MADELINE. *(On phone.)* Pete? Boy, you must be one tired boy, if you're not home yet. Anyway, sorry I missed your call, if I did. I went back to the Zen Palate to pick up my camera? That I left because I got so mad at your father? Anyway, I ran into Hank, and, well, what can I say? He's baaaaaaack. *(High voice.)* Help.

(MADELINE hangs up. PETE re-enters and looks at the telephone.)

PETE. Oh fuck.

TIM. *(From offstage.)* Hey! Bronco Billy! What's goin' on!

PETE. Nothing. Be right there.

(PETE exits back into the bedroom.)

(End of Scene)

(Two hand puppets—MAN and WOMAN. The woman hand puppet is the MADELINE puppet. The MAN puppet should be wearing a Patriots hat and a jersey from another team.)

MAN. We can fuck just as soon as this football game is over with.

(WOMAN PUPPET reaches behind and comes up with an Oreo in her mouth.)

(Blackout. Lights up and a real man, HANK, sitting on the couch, holding the tv remote—he is wearing a Patriots hat and a jersey. Next to him is MADELINE, eating an oreo.)

HANK. *(To the TV.)* Go, go, GO! You asshole! *(Hates the play.)* Oh man. *(To MADELINE.)* Did you see that? The safety was right there—he was right THERE! *(Back to the game.)* Oh, I can't believe it—they're going to kick! NOOOOOOO! Just run it—you're right there! I can't watch. *(He does.)* FUUUUCK!

(HANK throws the remote down.)

MADELINE. *(Picking up the remote and trying to turn off the tv.)* I can't seem to get it to work now. There.

(TV off.)

HANK. Oh man. Fucking Patriots—why do I fall for it? *(To MADELINE.)* What? Did you turn it off? Give me that! Are you nuts? *(Grabs the remote and turns the tv back on.)* This remote is fucked. *(Not taking his eyes off the tv, he reaches for MADELINE—she snuggles close—he gives her a peck, then drops her for the tv.)* I think the switch on your remote is faulty, Babe.

MADELINE. I've long suspected it.

HANK. *(To the tv.)* Oh NO! Not again, you fucking dick. You Dick!

(Phone rings. MADELINE picks it up. We see PETE on the other end.)

PETE. Whatcha doin?

MADELINE. Hank's here.

HANK. *(To the tv.)* Oooooo, that's it. That's it, baby.

PETE. Yikes! Sorry.

(PETE hangs up.)

MADELINE. No! Don't hang up.

(MADELINE dials the phone.)

HANK. *(To the tv.)* Go, baby, go, go, go! Yes! Yes! Yesssssssss! *(PETE picks phone up.)* I'm comin'! I'm comin'!

MADELINE. Don't hang up!

PETE. This is too weird for me.

HANK. *(To the tv.)* I'm in there! Yes!

MADELINE. Peter—don't hang up, whatever you do, I want to—

HANK. *(To the tv.)* I'm in the pocket, baby! I'm there! I'm there! YESSSSSSSSSSSS! At last!! You're beautiful. You're beautiful.

PETE. Madeline?

MADELINE. He's watching football.

PETE. *While* he's doing it?

MADELINE. No, instead of doing it.

HANK. Who you talking to, Babe?

MADELINE. Peter.

HANK. *(About a player on tv.)* Oh, not this fucking guy. *(To the telephone.)* Hey, Pete—how's it hanging?

PETE. Tell Hank I appreciate his interest in the position of my willie, and that I would inquire about the relative positioning of his at this moment, but I fear I would know the answer, making his reply redundant.

(This cracks MADELINE up.)

MADELINE. *(To HANK.)* Pete says hi.

HANK. *(Not pleased at the laughter.)* Yea. *(Back to the game.)* Oh man... Go for it go for it got for it—FUCK MEEEEEE!

PETE. The ironic thing is that he doesn't mean it.

MADELINE. I know, it is a stupid relationship, but it is the only one I've got.

HANK. Half-time. *(To MADELINE.)* Don't get off the phone—I'm going out for a couple of grinders. Bring you back a tuna? *(He kisses her.)* Baby baby baby. Oooooo.

MADELINE. Yeah.

(HANK exits.)

PETE. What the fuck are you doing? Haven't we been down this road before?

MADELINE. Can't I have love?

PETE. He manipulates you. He turns you on a dime.

MADELINE. Do you even know where my fucking dime is?

PETE. Madeline! *(It hurt.)* Ooo. You got me there.

(Really long pause.)

MADELINE & PETE. It's just that— No, you go—, No, I'll—

PETE. It's your life—you talk.

MADELINE. You're right, Peter. It is my life. You are also right about Hank—you were, as I recall, right the last time.

PETE. He does look great in Levis.

MADELINE. I know.

PETE. Don't get hurt.

MADELINE. Peter...

PETE. All right. Get hurt. Call me. Watch your butt.

MADELINE. I have to do something! I'm tired of love with batteries. I'm tired of my own hand. Sometimes I feel like a puppeteer. *(Making her hand a person—a la Senor Wences, she talks to it.)* "Was it good for you?" *(Hand speaks back.)* "Yes, it was!"

PETER. Did you just talk to your hand?

MADELINE. Yes, is that a bad sign?

PETER. No worse than any of the others.

MADELINE. I'll be all right.

PETER. You'll be all right.

MADELINE. God, we sound like a seminar.

PETER. Uh... I have a boyfriend—I think.

MADELINE. Oh my god.

PETER. Yes.

MADELINE. What's he like?

PETER. He's great, but it's still new—I don't want to jinx it.

MADELINE. You won't. Just be yourself. Bless you and him.

PETER. You're such a better person than I am.

MADELINE. Oh my god. Get a grip. Peter. You're turning into the Pillsbury Dough Boy. Look, Hank will be coming back any minute now. Call me tonight—no, don't call me tonight—hopefully, I'll be busy unless ESPN has captured Hank's attention again. I want to hear all about the guy—whatever you want to divulge—okay?

PETER. Okay. Bye.

MADELINE. Bye.

(They hang up.)

MADELINE. Oh, Peter, why do you get to be in love?

(HANK re-enters.)

MADELINE. You're back quick. Where are the sandwiches?

HANK. I had to come back to ask you: How come I never make you laugh like that?

MADELINE. Like what?

HANK. Like Peter does.

MADELINE. You do make me laugh, you do make me laugh. You make me laugh a lot—you're a very funny man—humor isn't everything. I mean, there's a lot of a relationship that has nothing to do with laughing, believe me. Believe me, laughter is not what you want, you know, you know, at the height of passion. I mean, you know, *irony* is the death of erotic feeling. They can't really exist in the same space, you know, Hank.

HANK. I'm a sex object.

MADELINE. No, you're not! Well, yeah, you are! You are a mighty sex object. Yeah.

HANK. You're using me.

MADELINE. I love you. I am hot for you. You are a wonderful man.

HANK. Okay. Two nuns walk into a bar.

MADELINE. Yeah.

HANK. And one says—I can tell by your face that you won't think this is funny.

MADELINE. Of course I will.

HANK. No, that's what the nun said. *(MADELINE laughs.)* See? You laugh harder at fucking Pete just looking at you than you do at a joke from me.

MADELINE. Tell me a better joke, Hank, and I'll laugh more.

HANK. Okay. A guy goes hunting, see? And he sees this huge bear and gets him in his sights and shoots him and the bear falls down, dead. So the hunter is jubilant—man, he is so pleased with himself. He runs down to where the bear fell and the damn bear is gone. Suddenly, he feels this tap on his shoulder and turns around and there's the bear—huge mother—fucking grizzly. "Blow me," says the bear. So the hunter is afraid for his life and he makes himself do it. He sucks the bear off and the bear runs off and the hunter goes back to camp and barfs, but he is so mad, he's even more determined to get this bear. So the next day, he goes out and, sure enough, he sees the same bear rambling through the woods, so he gets him in his sights and blam, blam, blam! Shoots him several times. The bear falls and the hunter runs there. But when he gets there, the damn bear is nowhere to be seen. And then, he feels that tap on his shoulder. He turns around and there's the bear, but this time, the bear says, "Turn around and drop your pants." So the hunter does and the bear fucks him in the butt, nearly tearing him apart. The hunter drags himself back to camp and sits in a cold stream and thinks about revenge. The next day, the hunter goes out with his biggest gun. He looks for the bear all day, and, at about evening, he spies the bear at the stream. The hunter empties his gun into the bear, sees him fall, and runs down to finally get his prize. Sure enough, when he gets there, the bear is gone. Just as the hunter's about to give up, he feels this tap on his shoulder. He turns and, yes, it's the bear looking him right in the eye and saying, "You didn't come to hunt."

(MADELINE laughs a lot at this one.)

MADELINE. That is so funny, Hank. I love that.
HANK. It's a homo joke. I heard it from Pete a year ago.
MADELINE. Yeah, but delivery means a lot. *(She sits on his lap.)* And you, Hank, you deliver.

(He embraces her, but we see his face—he's not completely happy.)

HANK. Yeah. Old Hank—the delivery man.

(End of Scene)

(PETE and his father, CHARLIE, are on vacation. They are outside in the sun. CHARLIE isn't having a good time.)

PETE. Dad—

CHARLIE. I'm fine.

PETE. Dad—

CHARLIE. Where's that ring I gave you? You didn't lose it, did you?

PETE. No, I left it at home, so I wouldn't lose it on vacation.

CHARLIE. *(About someone staring at him.)* Oh god.

PETE. Dad, relax. It's very beautiful here. It's a very beautiful place. And history as long as your arm.

CHARLIE. Put your arms down. What are you doing with your arms. Good God, do you want somebody to come over?

PETE. Maybe. *(CHARLIE looks incredulously at PETE.)* Dad, you picked this vacation! Without ever consulting me! And I love it—I love *that.* That you picked it.

CHARLIE. I didn't know!

PETE. Of course you didn't. Believe me, I know that.

CHARLIE. I mean, it's just that—you know, son—I've made my peace—no, that's wrong—I've *long ago,* accepted Your—Your—

(STAVROS enters, smiles at them.)

STAVROS. *(Greek accent.)* 'Ello. Don't fight. Love.

(STAVROS exits.)

CHARLIE. *(To exiting STAVROS.)* Listen! This is my *son*!

PETE. Dad, just look at this architecture. Isn't it beautiful? Like a storybook.

CHARLIE. ... Yeah...

PETE. I wonder what Mykonos means in Greek?

CHARLIE. I have an idea.

PETE. You know, sex is prurient to you.

CHARLIE. What do you mean? I loved sex with your mother.

PETE. Dad! Spare me.

CHARLIE. Aha. Gotcha.

PETE. What do you mean?

CHARLIE. My sex with your mother—WHICH CREATED YOU, I might add—is prurient to you. Whatever the hell "prurient" means.

PETE. It's not normal for children to enjoy hearing about the sex their parents have.

CHARLIE. Normal?

(CHARLIE gestures to take in their surroundings.)

PETE. Oh Dad, are we going to have this fucking fight again?

CHARLIE. Watch your mouth, Peter.

(STAVROS re-enters.)

STAVROS. You still angry? Fight? Nooooo. Bad. Most bad. Island of love. Many hunks. You American hunks. Huh? *(To PETE.)* Older man—good. *(To CHARLIE.)* Younger man— most good. I have love: gone.

PETE. Oh, did he... die?

STAVROS. Die? I wish die. Prick left me. German prick. Why do I love people I hate? Greek way—love/hate—who knows? Slavery, love—better to fuck pillow. Your hand. Hand never leave you. Hand never talk back. *(PETE laughs to himself.)* Why you laugh? Stavros funny?

PETE. No. It's—I was thinking of something, I—

STAVROS. What?

PETE. Just some—my friend Madeline talks to her hand. And it talks back.

CHARLIE. What?!

PETE. *(To CHARLIE.)* Just one night we were talking on the phone, and Madeline cracked me up with talking to her hand you had to be there, I guess.

STAVROS. You have a funny sister?

PETE. No, Madeline is—Madeline—she's... my... friend.

STAVROS. You have girlfriend, too? *(To CHARLIE.)* You watch him.

CHARLIE. He's my son. *(To everyone in hearing distance.)* He's my SON!!!!

STAVROS. Americans. Who are you? Anybody know over there? You bring slaves over. Now they yell at you. Your women are, are wild—touch themselves and talk to hands. Indians used to love fight—(Mimes arrow leaving bow.)— now they dress like cowboy. What happened to cowboys? I loved them. Cowboys here, but not real. Don't know horse from mo-ped. From big dog with long hair they comb and comb and walk around—hate dogs. America all gone. New name—you need new name. Greece—always same. Thousands of year—the same.

(DALE enters, played by actress who plays MOTHER.)

DALE. Excuse me, I'm with a tour over there, and I couldn't help overhearing. I know it's none of my business, but I'm from Duluth, and we'd like to say that America is not all gone and our name is fine.

CHARLIE. Wow.

DALE. And if it wasn't for us confused Americans, who would buy your t-shirts, sir?

CHARLIE. Yes!

PETE. Yikes.

DALE. And I'm a little fuzzy on World War II, but I think we saved your butts.

PETE. Oh god.

CHARLIE. That's right!

STAVROS. *(To PETE.)* You want get laid?

PETE. No! I mean, good lord! Dad—

CHARLIE. *(To DALE.)* My name is Charles Szczepanek, and this is my son.

STAVROS. What?

DALE. Hello. I'm Dale Williamson. I'm from Duluth.

(STAVROS exits.)

CHARLIE. Peter. Look Ms. Williamson. Could I buy you a drink?

DALE. All right. Sure. *(To her crowd.)* Girls!

PETER. Look, Dad. I've got a headache. I'm going to lie down—I'll see you at dinner. *(CHARLIE gives him a look.)* Dad. I Have a Headache. I also have Taste. Excuse me, Mrs. Williamson—

DALE. Call me Dale.

PETER. Perhaps I'll see you later.

(PETER exits.)

DALE. Nice boy.

CHARLIE. Well, aren't you a breath of fresh air.

DALE. We're all going to this place on the dock—you want to come, Mr.—ah—

CHARLIE. Szczepanek. Call me Charlie.

DALE. Charlie.

CHARLIE. You got any Polish people in Duluth?

DALE. Oh, we've got everything in Duluth.

(CHARLIE and DALE exit.)

(End of Scene)

(Lights up on PETE, fumbling with his room key. STAVROS steps out of the darkness.)

STAVROS. Peter.

PETE. Oh.

STAVROS. I'm sorry. I'm a fool.

PETE. My father—

STAVROS. Beautiful man. Like you.

PETE. I resemble my mother, actually—they say.
STAVROS. Peter—
PETE. I have a lover.
STAVROS. What do you think life is? You find a place you like, someone you like, you say, not now, I be back, very beautiful, very perfect, not now, I be back, I be back this way, not this time, another time, this time not right, another time, I be back, I embrace you then, I kiss you then, I hold you then, not now, another time, I be back. But no, no one come back, ever. Greece here thousand of year. Stavros her thirty five. No one come back. Ever. Now is only time. Now. Now, Peter who resemble his mother. Now.

(STAVROS kisses PETER.)

PETE. I—
STAVROS. Now.

(End of Scene)

(MADELINE is in a girl bar. An older woman, DORIS, walks by and cruises her, exits. MADELINE crosses to a stool and sits. Music starts and MADELINE looks up and stares at some entertainment. It shocks and transfixes her. The music is quite erotic. She stares. DORIS comes up and gives MADELINE a glass of white wine.)

DORIS. Yes, those are female go-go dancers. And, yes, this is a dyke bar. And, yes, that is a nice glass of Chablis. And I'm a nice dyke and—are you from Minneapolis or something?

MADELINE. Queens.

DORIS. Haven't been out in a while. I know how it feels. They're very young, aren't they? Lots and lots of tight little butts and upturned breasts. I mean the whole bar—not just the dancers. Now, check this out. *(Shouts to dancer we don't see.)* Sabrina!

(Music is belly-dancing music.)

DORIS. It's a real belly-dance.

(MADELINE watches, mouth open.)

MADELINE. She's wonderful.

DORIS. I know.

MADELINE. How does she do that?

DORIS. She started young. In her uncle's restaurant.

MADELINE. And he let her?

DORIS. He did more than that.

MADELINE. It's just so—it's just so—I mean, we're all women, and she's doing these movements.

DORIS. Thousands of years—only for men. Now for us.

MADELINE. I mean, it's so, I don't know—like watching yourself do— *(Another amazing movement from Sabrina.)* Now that's just bad for her back.

DORIS. It's so effective, though. Good lord.

MADELINE. But—but—

DORIS. Doris.

MADELINE. Doris, didn't we condemn all of this in the seventies or whenever, I mean, we're close to the same age, I think—

DORIS. Fifty.
MADELINE. Fifty? I don't believe that.
DORIS. Yes.
MADELINE. You look wonderful.
DORIS. Thanks.
MADELINE. I mean—
DORIS. Just "thanks."
MADELINE. It's just that—I don't know why I'm here.
DORIS. Oh god. Why me?
MADELINE. I'm sorry. I—
DORIS. Drink your wine.

(MUSIC ends and Sabrina's dance—offstage applause and whistles.)

MADELINE. Are they whistling at her?
DORIS. No, the go-go dancers are coming back.
MADELINE. They're wearing—they have—
DORIS. Cocks, I know.
MADELINE. Why, Doris?
DORIS. Just think of it as another aspect of our mysterious sexuality. I mean, men have worn false breasts for hundreds of years—on television, prime time! In front of children, even. And male drag queens have tucked their genitals up so they can dress in tight Las Vegas Showgirl drag. Girls are wearing cocks, as part of their male drag gear.
MADELINE. But that one is in a little cocktail dress.
DORIS. I know. I have a little trouble...
MADELINE. It is erotic.
DORIS. That it is.
MADELINE. You explained it well.

DORIS. I'm trying to embrace it. I'm—I'm—I'm actually very old and trying to be Miranda about the whole thing: "Oh, brave new world that hath such creatures in it." Of course, what does Miranda know? She was living on an island with her weird father, a fairy, and a talking missing link who tried to rape her. In short, she could be my neighbor on West 57th Street.

MADELINE. Have you had dinner?

DORIS. I don't know.

MADELINE. I'm not really here because... I'd understand, if you said...

DORIS. Uh-huh.

MADELINE. I just know a lot of good restaurants. I eat out a lot. *(Pause.)* I have no idea what I'm doing.

DORIS. Oh, I know that. *(She scans bar for another prospect, fails.)* Come on.

(They exit.)

(End of Scene)

(PETE is running on the beach at Mykonos, looking for his father. It's night. The surf is pounding.)

PETE. Dad, dammit, where are you? DAD! DAD! Shit. Damn. What am I doing? He's a grown man. I'm a grown man. *(Looks at his watch.)* It's almost five o'clock in the morning! *(He stops to catch his breath and prays.)* Father, find my father.

(Beat. CHARLIE enters quietly. He's more than tipsy.)

CHARLIE. Pete? Jeez.
PETE. Dad? Dad!

(PETE runs to him but stops before he hugs him.)

CHARLIE. What are you doing out here? You're not with that slimy Greek, are you?
PETE. Dad! Christ!
CHARLIE. You been walking? I been walking. *(Peering up the hill.)* That our hotel? Yay. I knew that.
PETE. I was so worried when I realized I had no way to find you.
CHARLIE. Found.
PETE. How was Whatshername? Gail?
CHARLIE. Dale from Duluth.
PETE. How was she?
CHARLIE. Desperate. She was a desperate woman. She scared me. Like standing on the edge of a well—your cock about the size of a Vienna sausage—knowing that you could fall in at any moment and no one would hear your screams. *(Suddenly unsteady.)* Oh man.
PETE. Dad—
CHARLIE. I'm gonna—I gonna sit. *(CHARLIE sort of falls and lays there.)* Peter, the stars. Come down.

(PETE lays down next to CHARLIE.)

PETE. Beautiful.
CHARLIE. You know, I'm really lonely all the time. Lonely, lonely.
PETE. There's Sirius, Dad.

CHARLIE. Yeah. Sorry.

PETE. No, just look up there. That start—it's the Dog Star.

CHARLIE. What's it for? Ugly girls to wish on?

PETE. Are you sure we're related?

CHARLIE. You are my son! That's not funny. *(Tries to sit up.)* Whoa. *(Lies back down, sees star.)* It's bright.

PETE. Are you sure you're looking at the right star?

CHARLIE. Oh, who cares? I'm sorry, what's it for, Peter? Love?

PETE. No, just heat, Dad. And good harvest. And he rising of the Nile. That's what it's for.

CHARLIE. The Nile rises, the heat comes, and we chase after Duluth babes. Some star comes out, some river rises, and we make fools of ourselves. It's too beautiful here. Let's go back to New York. I need a body with multiple stab wounds. Help me.

(PETE helps his father stand.)

CHARLIE. If your mother could see me now.

PETE. It's all right, Dad.

CHARLIE. If your mother could see me now.

PETE. Dad.

CHARLIE. If she could see me now, I'd be saved. You need somebody to watch you live.

PETE. Don't tell me that, Dad.

CHARLIE. Okeedoke. *(A confession.)* I love Madeline, son.

PETE. So do I, Dad.

(Pause.)

CHARLIE. Right.

(They exit.)

(End of Scene)

(JACKIE is exhausted and lying down in the subway tunnel or under a culvert or in a terrible SRO where lots of human fighting can be heard. He had his shirt off.)

JACKIE. Don't be scared. Don't be worried. Hush, hush—everyone can just be quiet now. We've become friends now, so I can tell you. Ever since I was six years old, I have seen this...thing in the corners of whatever room I was sleeping in. I thought it was a spider, but it only had four legs, and it was white. Every year it seemed to get bigger and then I noticed that it had a head and two of the legs were arms. One night I saw this movie on tv called "Close Encounters of the Third Kind" and I just wanted to scream but I couldn't move, 'cause out of the spaceship came this thing that looked just like the thing in my room only the thing in the movie was a kind alien, just really, really, skinny and about 20 feet tall. The thing in my room isn't that tall and I know it's not kindly. It stares at me and I know it's a human thing, but not a guy because of no cock, but not a girl—no pussy—in fact, nothing between its legs, like some weird-ass doll, with spider arms. I'm almost eighteen and this thing is still hanging around in the dark, looking at me, and I'm terrified to sleep some nights. Even in the Holiday Inn, I've seen it. And I hope it's not here now because I really, really need to sleep. I really do. Go to sleep, Jackie. I

want you to go to sleep now. "Are you asleep in there? Jack?"
Go to sleep. Go to sleep now. Hush, hush, hush—shhhhhhh.
Very quiet now. Just let go please. Just— *(His eyes are closed
and he's breathing softly. We think he's fallen asleep. His eyes
open.)* Please.

(End of Scene)

*(PETER is back from his trip—his suitcase is open. TIM and
     PETER have just made love.)*

TIM. Now, what else did you bring me?

PETER. I can't believe how happy I am now. Do you know
how hard it is to be in some romantic place without you?

(TIM reaches into PETER'S suitcase, finds something.)

PETER. Don't. That's for Maddy.

TIM. Can't I see?

PETER. It's wrapped.

TIM. Not well.

PETER. Don't, The wrapping is part of the funny story.
Here's your big present.

TIM. But it's small. *(Opens it.)* Oooooo. Nice.

PETER. We can have it sized. It's lapis lazuli.

TIM. Thanks, baby. *(Kisses him.)* No funny story to go with
this?

PETER. No... I could make something up.

TIM. You called Maddy from the Detroit airport.

PETER. I had that layover—flight from Hell.

TIM. Why didn't you call me, Peter?

PETER. It was two a.m.!

TIM. I need more sleep than Madeline?

PETER. I've called Madeline at two a.m. so many times—god.

(Beat.)

TIM. Peter. I am a gay man. I want a relationship with another gay man.

PETER. Well, you've got that.

TIM. You save things for her.

PETER. What? That gift? It's just a joke thing. What do you mean, I save "things" for Madeline?

TIME. You save little stories for her. And little jokes. And little things that you felt. You call her at two a.m. for Chrissake!

PETER. Tim—

TIM. *I* want to hear about your flight from hell! I can't tell you how many times you have said this to me, "I was telling Maddy this, and I realized how great that Mousaka was." And *then* you tell *me* about it. I want to hear about the Mousaka! I want the real raw Mousaka story before it goes through her!

PETER. Timothy, you're jealous of Madeline.

TIM. Damn right! How can I compete with a 20-year old relationship!

PETER. I love you.

TIM. You love her.

PETER. It's a different love.

TIM. You save things for her!

PETER. Here! Do you want the damn present I got for her?

TIM. OH, that's not it, and you know it!!

PETER. Tim, you are my lover.

TIM. Do you know what it's like to lie with someone in the dark, after you've made love, and realize that only part of them is really there? That, inside, they're secretly thinking of something funny that happened, that they can't share with you because it's about you?

PETER. When have I ever done that? Told Madeline anything about our sex life, for Chrissakes?

TIM. Oh, it doesn't have to be about our sex life—it can be about anything. Because you've known each other so long, everything anyone can think of has some reference, some story from the past, some poem, some fragment of a memory. You have this entire life with Madeline. And she's not even an ex-wife that I have a chance of supplanting. Nooooo. She's still here—right smack dab in the center of your life, still "Maddy", with both hands on this enormous, unchangeable, rock solid relationship of yours. Do you know why you haven't gotten a lover before now? You never really needed one. You just needed to get laid. You are in a celibate marriage with Madeline. The "marriage of true minds" already happened when you were sixteen.

PETER. Fourteen.

TIM. Jesus! Who can compete with that? Well, I *need* a marriage. In these fucking awful times. I need a marriage of true minds.

(Beat.)

PETER. Wow, Tim.

TIM. Right.

PETER. I can't give up my friendship with Madeline. I...
TIM. Just stop saving things for her. Save things for *me*.

(PETER opens MADELINE'S present, show it to TIM.)

PETER. It's a box of Greek tampons.
TIM. Oh man. Just what I always wanted. *(They laugh
weakly.)* Look, I'm sorry. *(TIM kisses PETER.)* I'm going to
take a shower. Then I'll take you out to eat some real American food—sushi.

*(TIM exits. Sound of a shower. The phone rings and PETER
looks at it, but lets the answering machine pick it up.)*

ANSWERING MACHINE *(PETER V.O.)* You have
reached 719-4320. I'm not back from my vacation, but Tim is
here and can take a message for me, so leave it after the beep.
Frank O'Hara will return with a new poetry selection soon.

*(Beep sounds. MADELINE'S voice comes through on the an-
swering machine. PETER just looks at the phone, but
doesn't pick it up.)*

MADELINE'S V.O. *(Through the answering machine.)*
Hello? Peter, where the fuck are you??!!! Life sucks!!!! I loved
your phone call from Detroit, but WHERE ARE YOU?????!!!
Tim, you needn't answer this hysterical message. Give Pete
my love when you talk to him. This is Madeline and she's
going MAAAAD! I can't believe you're not home yet. Are
you there? Are you there? Peter????? Okay. Bye. Byeeeeeeee.
God, I am so not funny without you. Bye.

(She hangs up. PETER puts his head in his hands.)

(End of Scene)

(DORIS and MADELINE are at MADELINE's apartment. DORIS is popping some Tums.)

MADELINE. I liked this Afghani place where we ate tonight better than that Thai place we went last week, didn't you? Although Thai food is easier to digest, I guess. Now there's a Venezuelan place near—well, I'm not sure, but I'll find out for next week. So what do you want to watch on TV tonight? Did you notice that guy at the door when I was getting my mail? I swear he was staring at us. But I could be just—is that a new shirt? I didn't notice before—

DORIS. Madeline—

MADELINE. It's good on you, the shirt. I mean—

DORIS. Just "thanks."

MADELINE. Where do you want to go next Thursday or Wednesday, it could be. It doesn't have to be Venezuelan and Pete can come with us, then—you've got to meet him—you two—

DORIS. Madeline—

MADELINE. Or maybe on the weekend.

DORIS. Madeline!

MADELINE. ...yeah...?

DORIS. You're a really nice woman, but—

MADELINE. Uh-oh.

DORIS. I don't think you feel "that way" about me.

MADELINE. Uh-oh.

DORIS. Look, darling. I'm too old to do therapy on someone and I've got plenty of friends. I hate to be crass, but I need
to get laid some time. If I can't, I'm spending tonight with my
VCR and a pint of Cherries Garcia.
    MADELINE. Oh.
    DORIS. I'm sorry.
    MADELINE. Okay.
    DORIS. You're really nice.
    MADELINE. Okay.
    DORIS. 'Bye.
    MADELINE. Okay. *(DORIS exits.)* Fine.

(End of Scene.)

(JACKIE is standing on a beach—we hear the surf.)

JACKIE. I had a baby sister who was born to see the future—she was born veiled, you know. The thing around her
face—the placenta. My mother is a Baptist, so she didn't want
to say it out loud, in front of the doctor or anything. But she
really did believe that it was a sign of future-seeing, and it is,
from way back. Then the baby died in a few hours, having
never even seen the sun, or a star. But I wonder, sometimes, if
she really did see the future. In the few short hours she lived.
And her little babiness couldn't take it—just couldn't take it.

*(An older man, SANNY, played by the MOTHER or the
    CHARLIE actor, enters—more androgynous than male,
    dressed badly and smoking.)*

SANNY. Who you talking to?

JACKIE. No one.

SANNY. I heard you talking.

JACKIE. It was nothing.

SANNY. You don't want to tell me. You think I'm old and weird. That's all right. That's all right. I give you your space. It's a big old beach. I come here for years. I'm a little boy over there. I'm a big boy over there behind those rocks. I'm an old man here. Huh? Huh? How old do you think I am?

JACKIE. Forty—eight—?

SANNY. I'm sixty-two.

JACKIE. Wow.

SANNY. Sixty-two years old. I've seen a lot. You a fairy?

JACKIE. I'm waiting for my girlfriend.

SANNY. Uh-huh. I seen the burning of Wonderland. Hours it burned. Nothing left. Midgets, bearded ladies, dog-faced boys and girls scurrying out with no place to go. No home. That's why Manhattan is so weird. They spawned, you know. Their blood is in all of us. I seen them kill an elephant. Fifteen minutes it took—one lethal injection after another and she wouldn't die. That blood is on our hands, too. Now Coney Island is filled with niggers on welfare. You look like James Dean.

JACKIE. Who's that? Oh. Oh, the dead guy. *(Starts to go.)* Look—

SANNY. Don't go. What'd I say? Fairy? Nigger? I'll be good. I'm from another generation—we don't know how to be police, sometimes. Hey. You talk to nobody just fine—you can talk to me. I'm more fun than nobody out there.

JACKIE. Okay.

SANNY. You an actor? You rehearsing?

JACKIE. No, I pretend they're people out there who watch me, and I talk to them.

SANNY. You a lonely boy. Like me. Putting on a show, huh?

JACKIE. Sometimes.

SANNY. I live up there. My mother died. Come with me? I've got some hamburger I'm gonna fry. I got a big screen tv.

JACKIE. You get cable?

SANNY. A hundred and two channels. Kids programs from Japan. Cooking in Egypt. Hindu movies.

JACKIE. Nature programs.

SANNY. Every minute somewhere. Come on. *(SANNY reaches out his hand.)* Hey. *(JACKIE shakes his hand.)* Nice ring there.

JACKIE. NYPD. My dad gave it to me.

SANNY. I'd better take good care of you.

(They exit.)

(End of Scene)

(The sound of an answering machine beep and PETE'S message.)

PETE'S V.O. You have reached Pete's answering machine. Leave a message after the beep. Please do not leave messages for Tim here. He can be reached at his old number. Thanks bye.

CHARLIE'S V.O. Pete? Pete, this your dad. I'm holding my father's 30-year ring that I gave to you. Mac took it off some street kid beaten unconscious in Coney. What the hell happened? Call me!

(End of Scene)

(MADELINE and PETE are at his apartment. It's raining outside.)

PETE. Sorry about the rain. No beach.

(PETE opens a Diet Coke.)

MADELINE. That's all right. I just feel like staying in. It's been a helluva year. *(He puts the Coke down. MADELINE reaches for the Diet Coke to drink from, but PETE picks it up again.)* What? Do you have cold? No biggie. *(PETE won't give her the can and she gets a little scared.)* Give me the can, Pete. Give me the can, Peter. No. No. No. *(Long beat.)* It's not carried in saliva.

PETE. I read something—saliva was on the list.

MADELINE. No, Peter, no. No. No, no, no, no, no, no, noooooooo.

PETE. I'm just Positive. It's no further than that.

(Long beat.)

MADELINE. No

PETE. If I take care of myself...

MADELINE. Looks like you already failed there! I'M NOT GONNA SAY I'M SORRY I SAID THAT. HOW COULD

YOU SURVIVE TEN YEARS AND THEN FUCK UP??!!!!!
YOU WERE SAFE, YOU WERE SAFE, GODDAMMIT!!!
YOU SURVIVED TEN YEARS! YOU SURVIVED
EVERYBODY! GOOD-BYE, BARRY! GOOD-BYE,
KEVIN! AND ALLEN AND SHAWN AND DAVID AND
JERRY. AND RON. AND BOB. AND STEWART. AND JOE.
And Chris. We saw everyone of them go!! You and me. We
sat in those awful pews and then chairs and then theatres and
listened to the handful of stories and the shreds of our friend's
lives and managed to get up and go on and live and you were
still safe and I thanked God every day that you were safe and
I'm a goddam atheist and you know it!! And all those years
when you were going to Fire Island, to those parties with your,
as you call it, non-macho body and your overdeveloped sense
of taste, and not getting laid and spending all your time talking
to some too-old queen in the kitchen while everyone is outside
fucking madly in the sand, and I kept worrying that you weren't
getting a date and it was not fair—Well, ever since this
FUCKING plague hit, I have been more and more grateful
that you have that "non-macho" body because nearly every
single person from those days is GONE, Peter! Dead, Peter.
And you're going to leave me in this stupid world to be wise
or something? And I'll be an old lady and make my peace and
thought I had a good life or whatever you say to the living to
make them feel better, and I will have found some way to be
happy some of the time, but it will all be without you. How in
the FUCK am I supposed to live without YOU??!!

PETER. I don't know how I got it. I was always very careful. Tim is negative.

MADELINE. Does Tim know?

PETER. Yeah.

MADELINE. What did he say?

PETER. He said, "How are you gonna tell Madeline?"

MADELINE. I'm not crying any more. I'm so sorry about... the yelling, Peter. I'm so sorry. I'm so sorry. I'm so sorry.

PETER. It's all right.

MADELINE. I'm only thinking of myself. When you really, really, really, really dread something, and it comes— Oh, Peter, our lives—your life.

PETER. We always wanted to have lives like in a novel.

MADELINE. Yeah, but by Noel Coward, not... Tolstoy.

PETER. Kafka.

MADELINE. It's not carried in saliva. GMHC says it's not carried in saliva.

PETER. Do you want to chance it?

(HE offers her the Diet Coke—she doesn't take it. He puts the Coke down. They both stare at it.)

(End of Scene)

(An Arapahoe man, very beautiful, is flying and holding JACKIE from behind. There's the sound of wind and the faint regular beep from a heart monitor.)

ARAPAHOE. *(Singing to himself. An Arapahoe song. A bit of country western. Something whizzes by.)* Uh-oh—time string. Jackie?

JACKIE. *(Waking up a bit.)* Uh?

ARAPAHOE. Awake?

JACKIE. I—...yeah.